The Boy Who Burped Too Much

LIBRARIAN REVIEWER

Laurie K. Holland

Media Specialist (National Board Certified), Edina, MN

MA in Elementary Education, Minnesota State University, Mankato, MN

READING CONSULTANT

Elizabeth Stedem

Educator/Consultant, Colorado Springs, CO

MA in Elementary Education, University of Denver, CO

Graphic Sparks are published by Stone Arch Books,
A Capstone Imprint
151 Good Counsel Drive, P.O. Box 669,
Mankato, Minnesota 56002.
www.capstonepub.com

Library of Congress Cataloging-in-Publication Data
Nickel, Scott.
   The Boy Who Burped Too Much / by Scott Nickel; illustrated by Steve Harpster.
   p. cm. — (Graphic Sparks)
   ISBN-13: 978-1-59889-037-2 (library binding)
   ISBN-10: 1-59889-037-9 (library binding)
   ISBN-13: 978-1-59889-168-3 (paperback)
   ISBN-10: 1-59889-168-5 (paperback)
   1. Graphic novels. I. Harpster, Steve. II. Title. III. Series.
PN6727.N544B69 2006
741.5—dc22   2005026693

Summary: Bobby Aaron was a cool kid, but not a normal kid. His burps were
uncontrollable. He belched at the movies, erupted in the library, and even blasted
away in the principal's office. Bobby needs to keep his cool and squelch his belches
in order to win the spelling bee. But then he runs into Courtney, another word for
"trouble." Gulp!

Art Director: Heather Kindseth
Production Manager: Sharon Reid
Production/Design: James Liebman, Mie Tsuchida
Production Assistance: Bob Horvath, Eric Murray

Printed in the United States of America in Stevens Point, Wisconsin.
032011
006120R

THE BOY WHO BURPED TOO MUCH

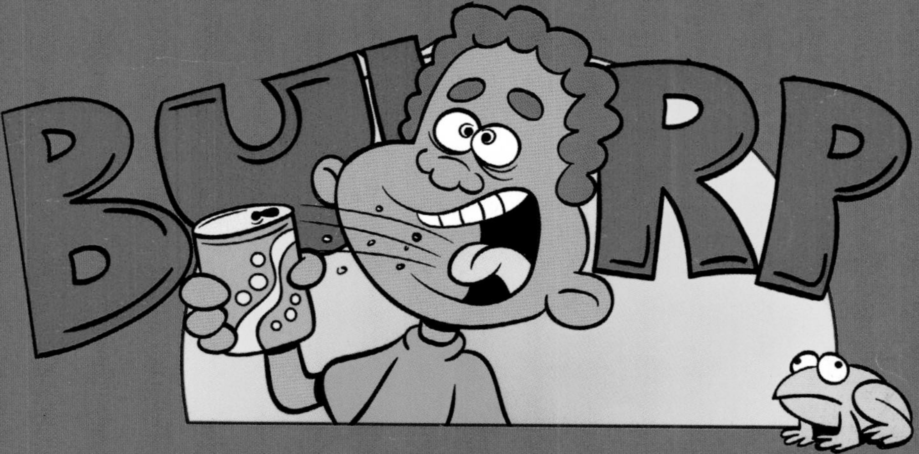
BURP

BY SCOTT NICKEL

ILLUSTRATED BY STEVE HARPSTER

STONE ARCH BOOKS
Minneapolis San Diego

CAST OF CHARACTERS

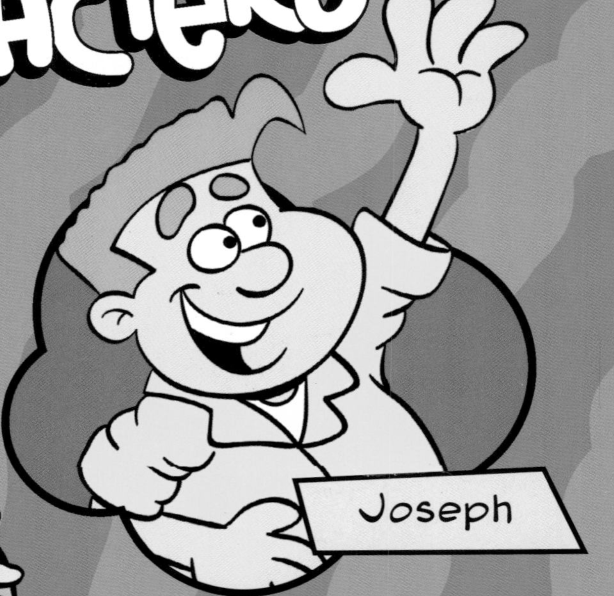

Joseph

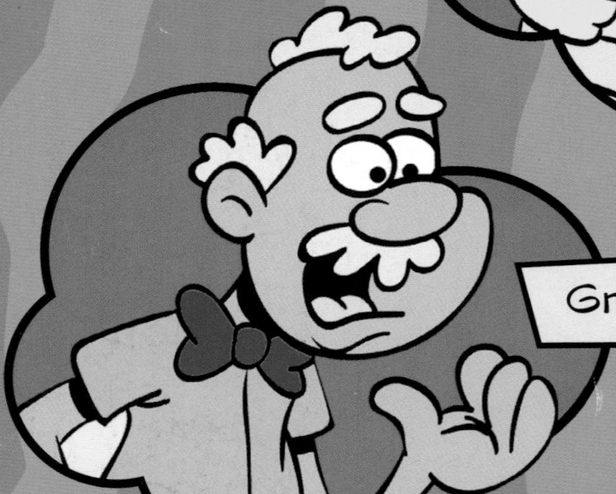

Grandpa

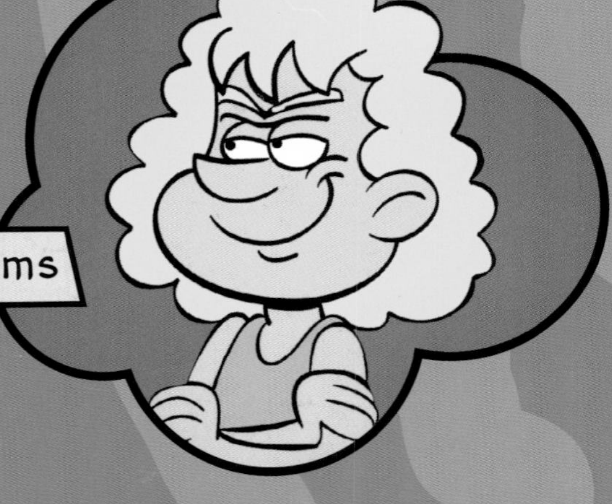

Courtney Williams

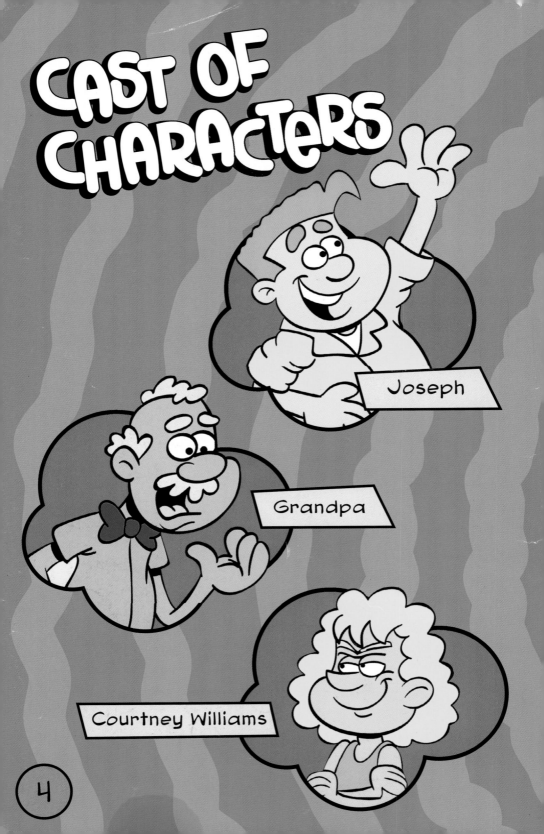

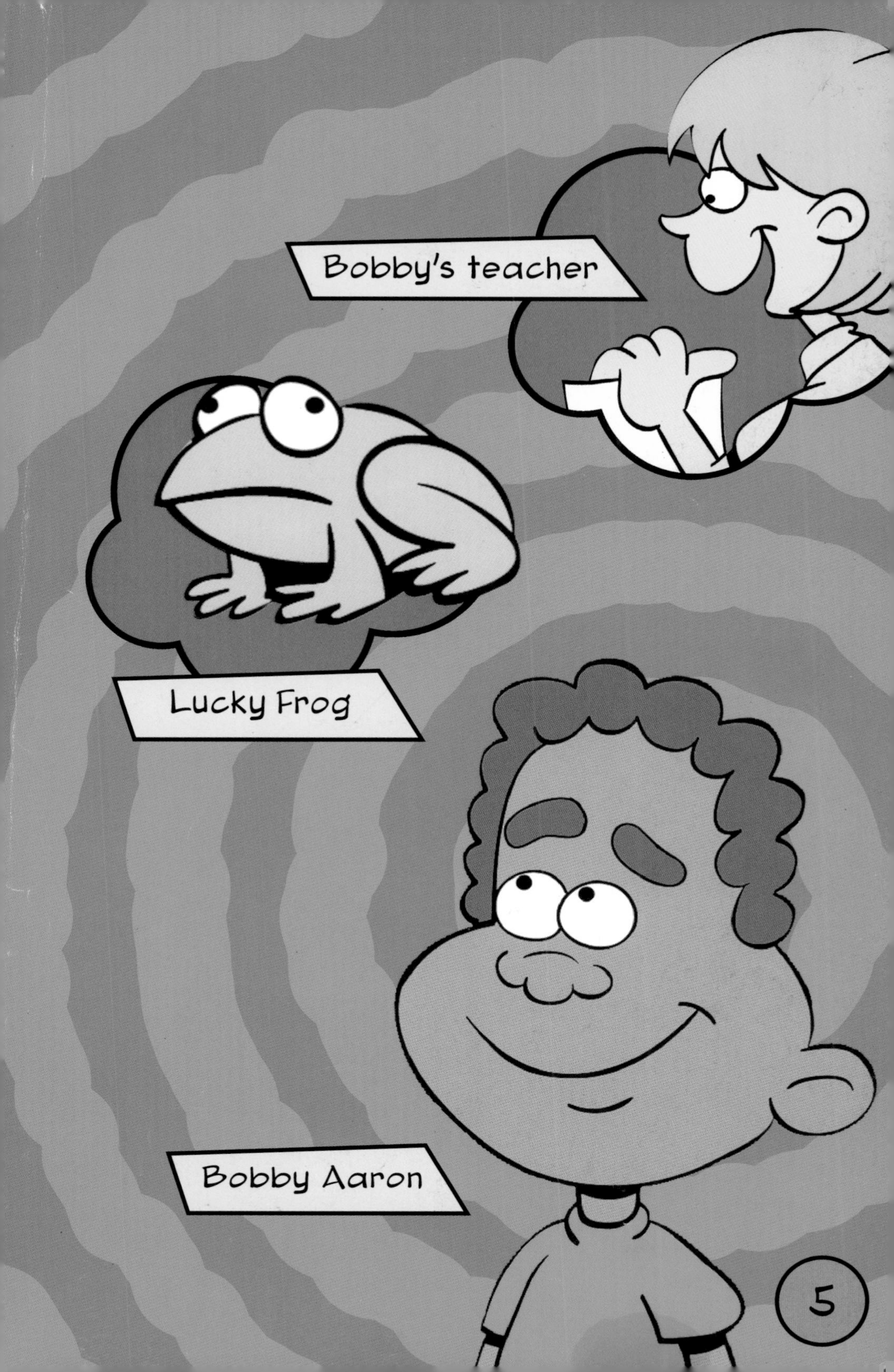
Bobby's teacher
Lucky Frog
Bobby Aaron

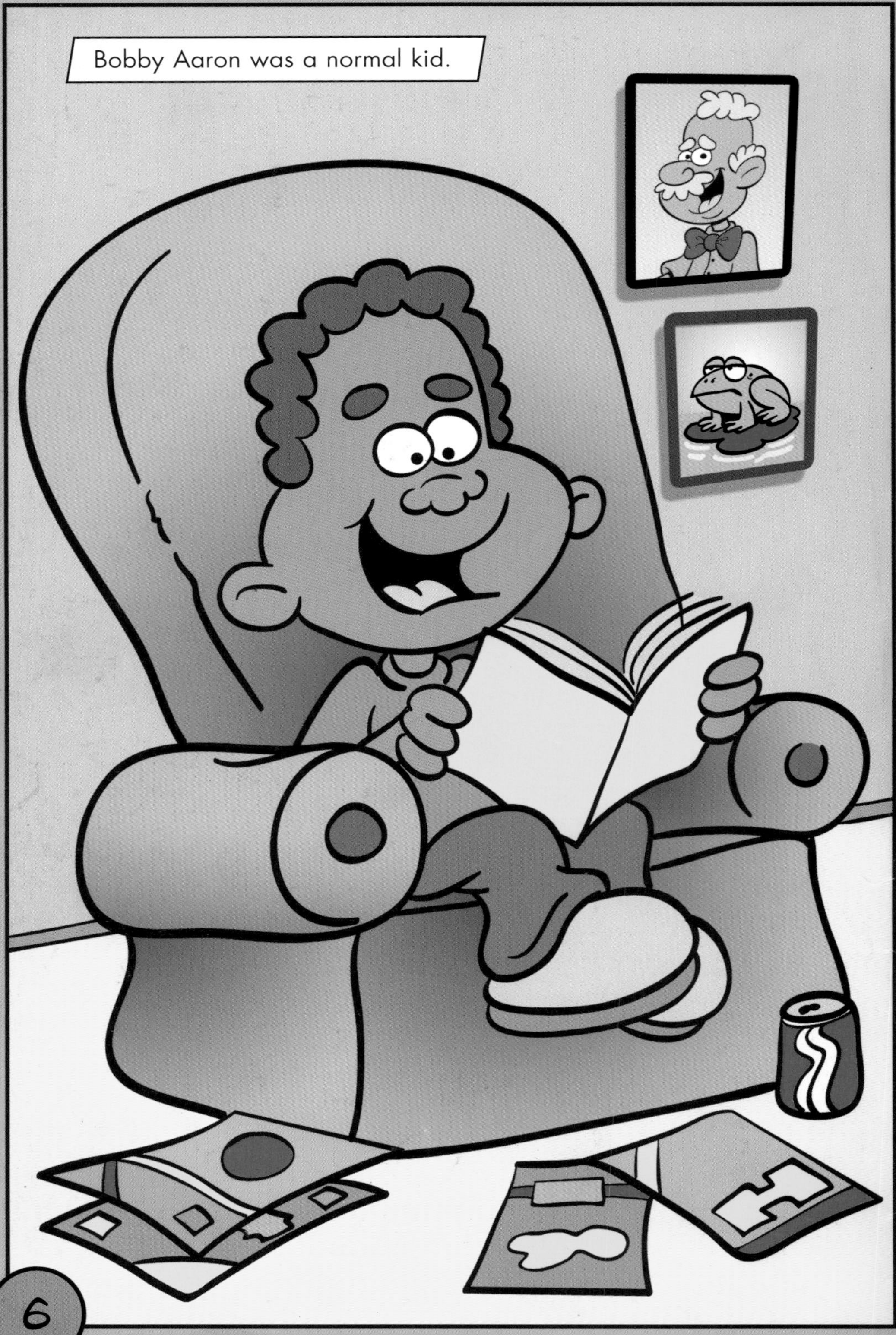
Bobby Aaron was a normal kid.

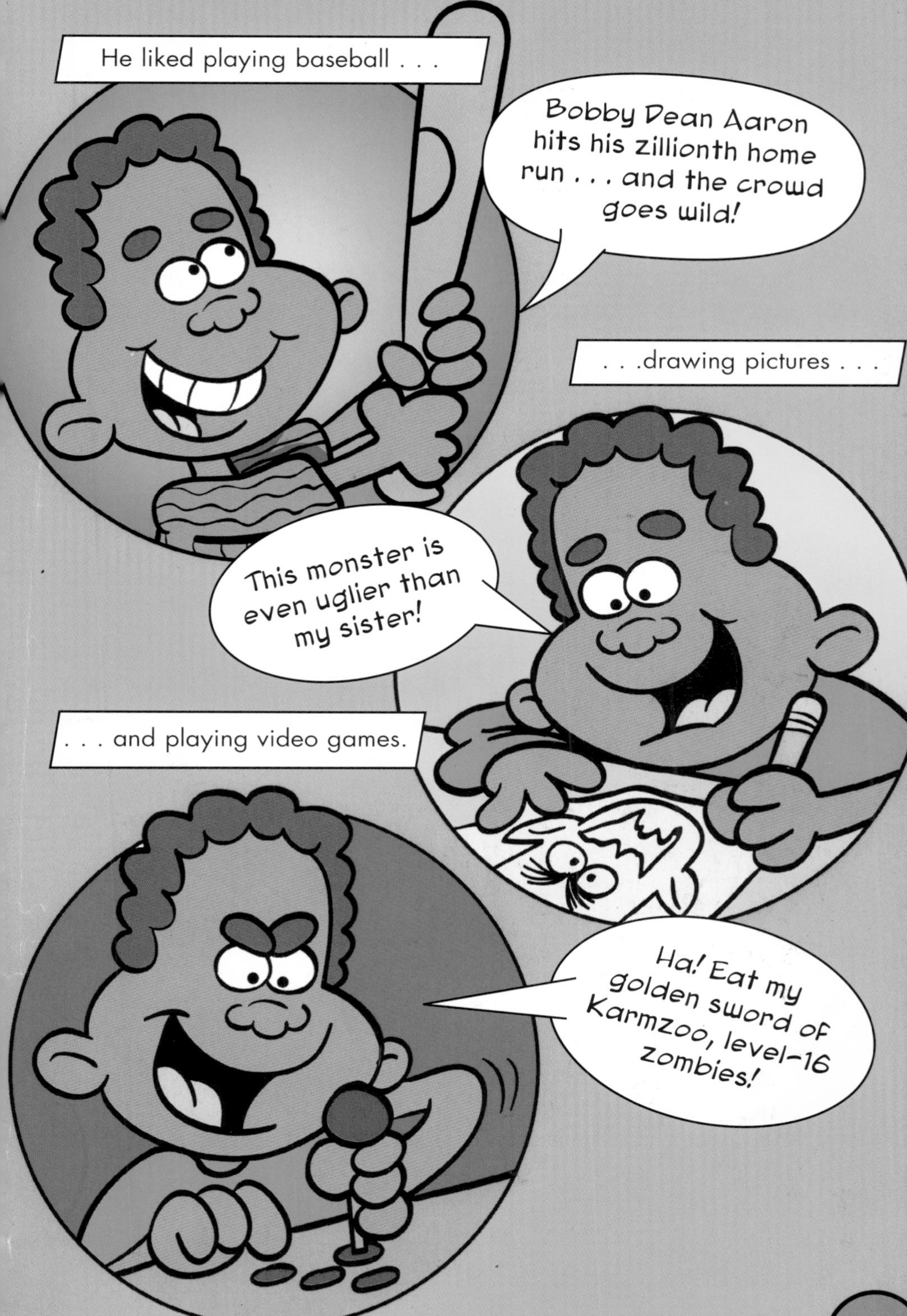
He liked playing baseball . . .
Bobby Dean Aaron hits his zillionth home run . . . and the crowd goes wild!
. . .drawing pictures . . .
This monster is even uglier than my sister!
. . . and playing video games.
Ha! Eat my golden sword of Karmzoo, level-16 zombies!

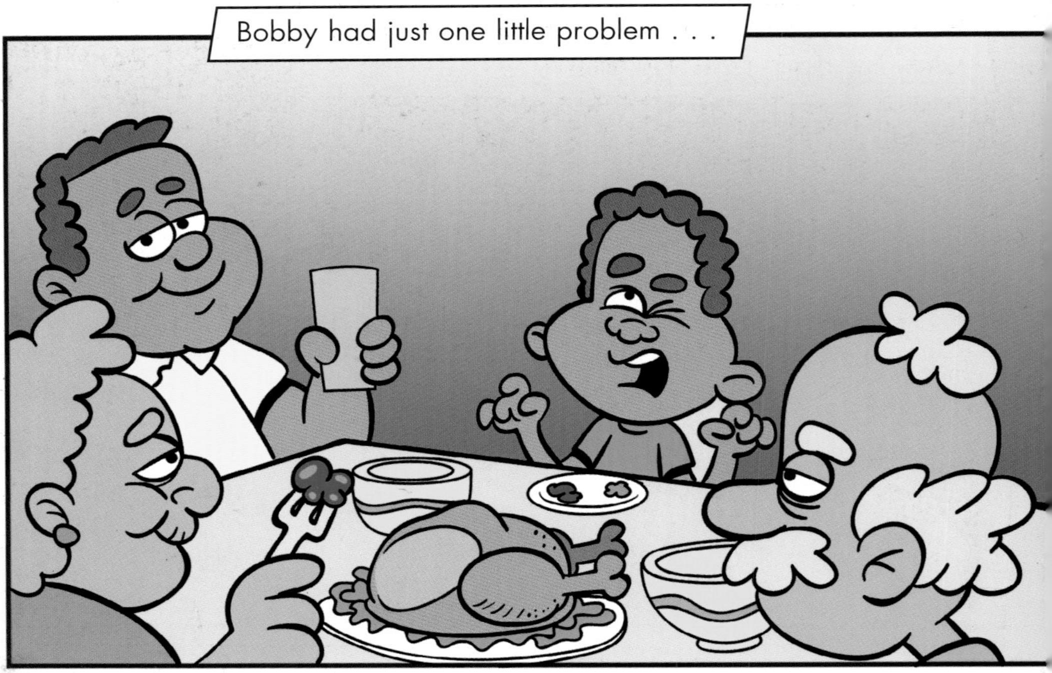
Bobby had just one little problem . . .

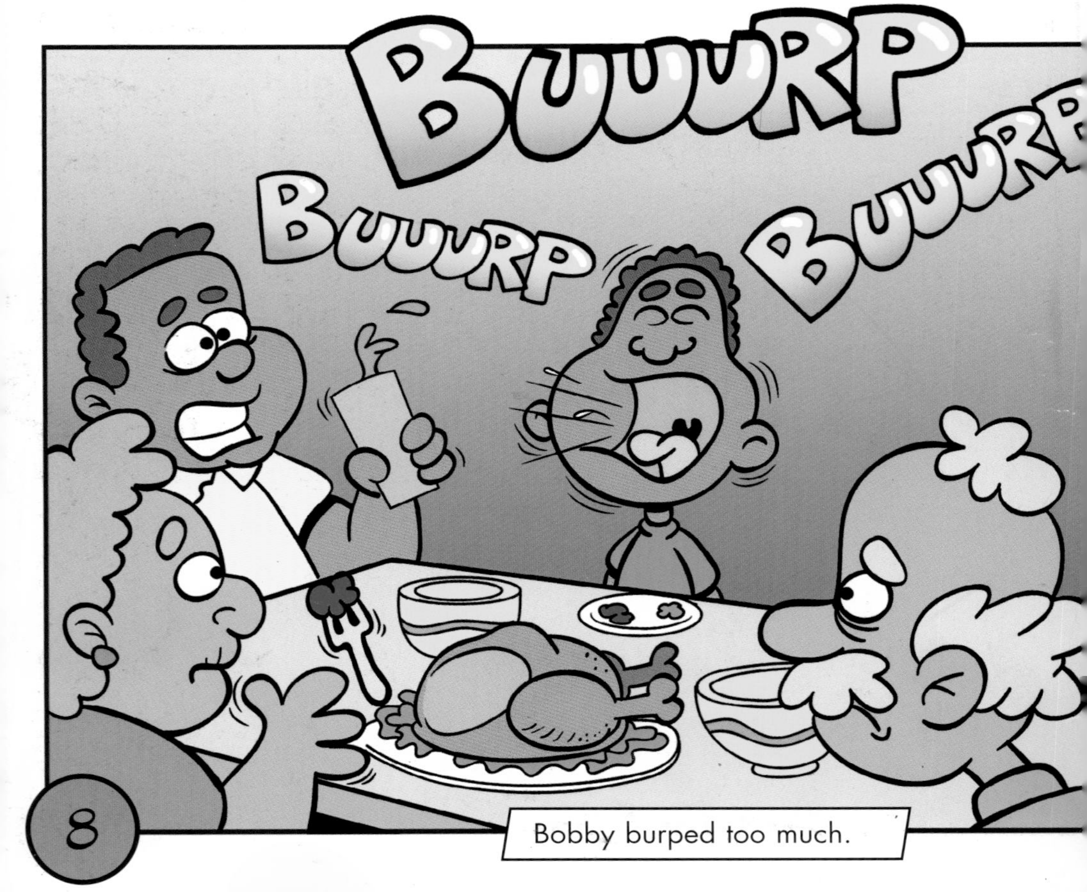
BUUURP
BUUURP
BUUURP
Bobby burped too much.

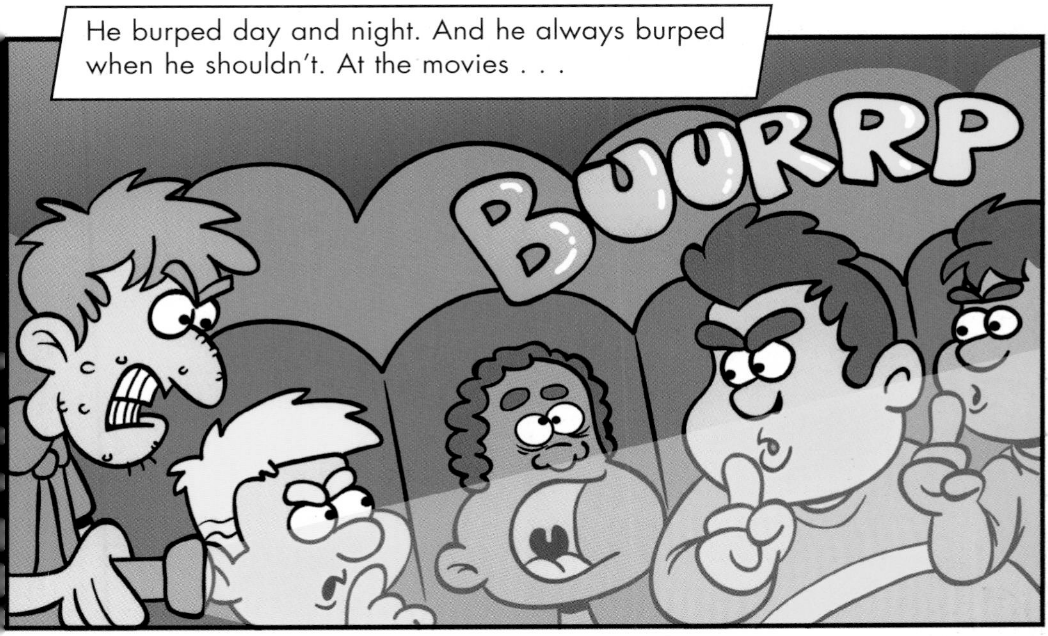
He burped day and night. And he always burped when he shouldn't. At the movies . . .
BUURRP

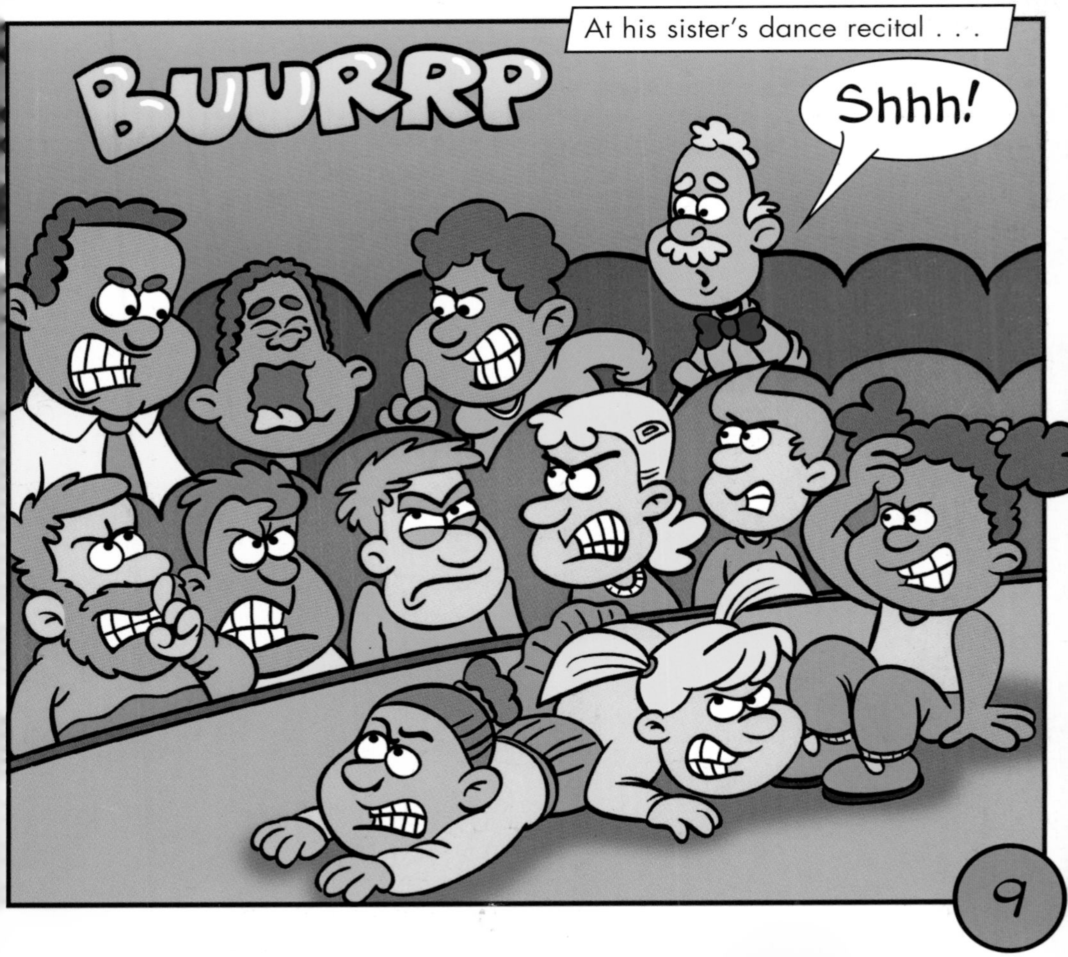
At his sister's dance recital . . .
BUURRP
Shhh!

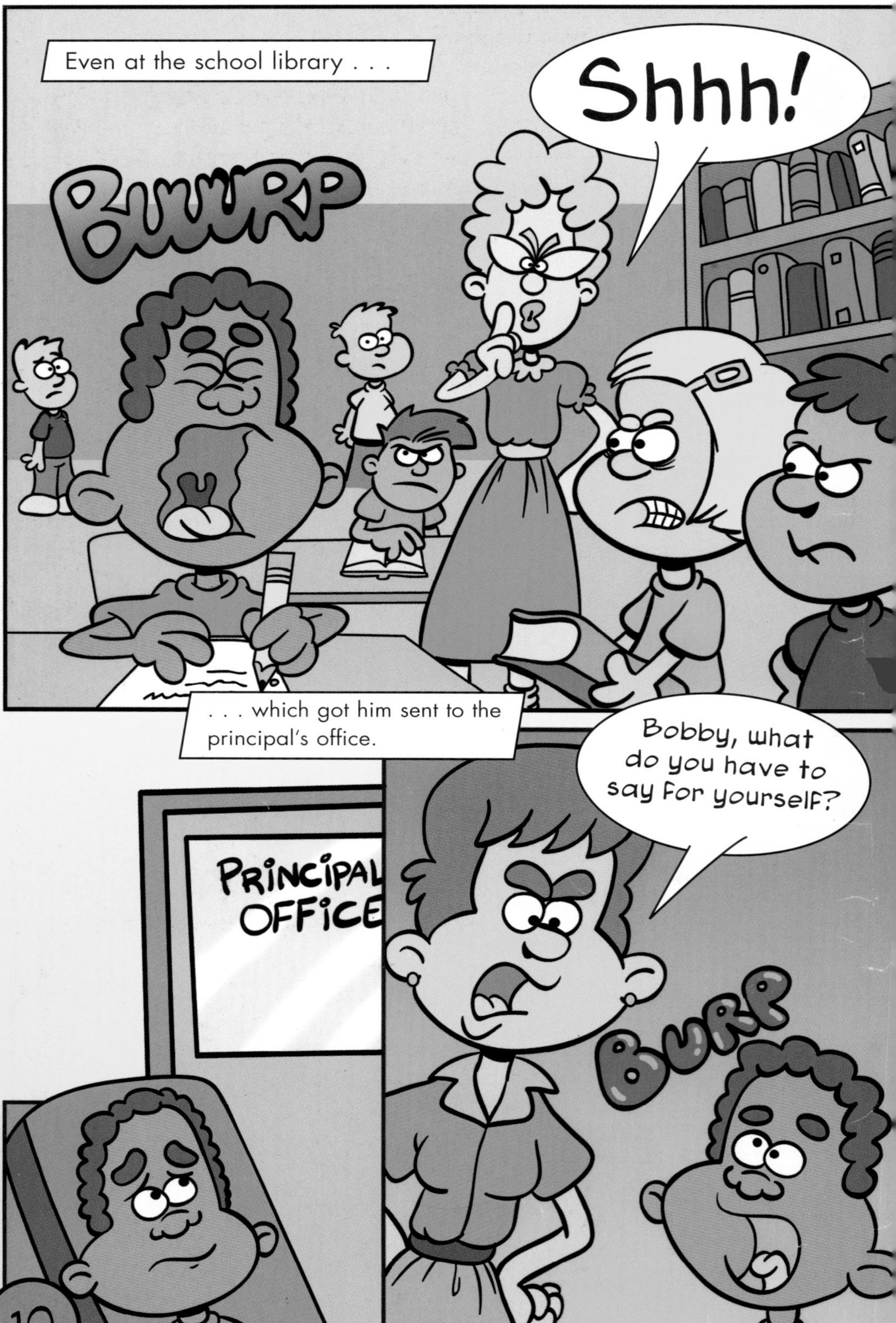
Even at the school library . . .
BUUURP
Shhh!
. . . which got him sent to the principal's office.
PRINCIPAL
OFFICE
Bobby, what do you have to say for yourself?
BURP

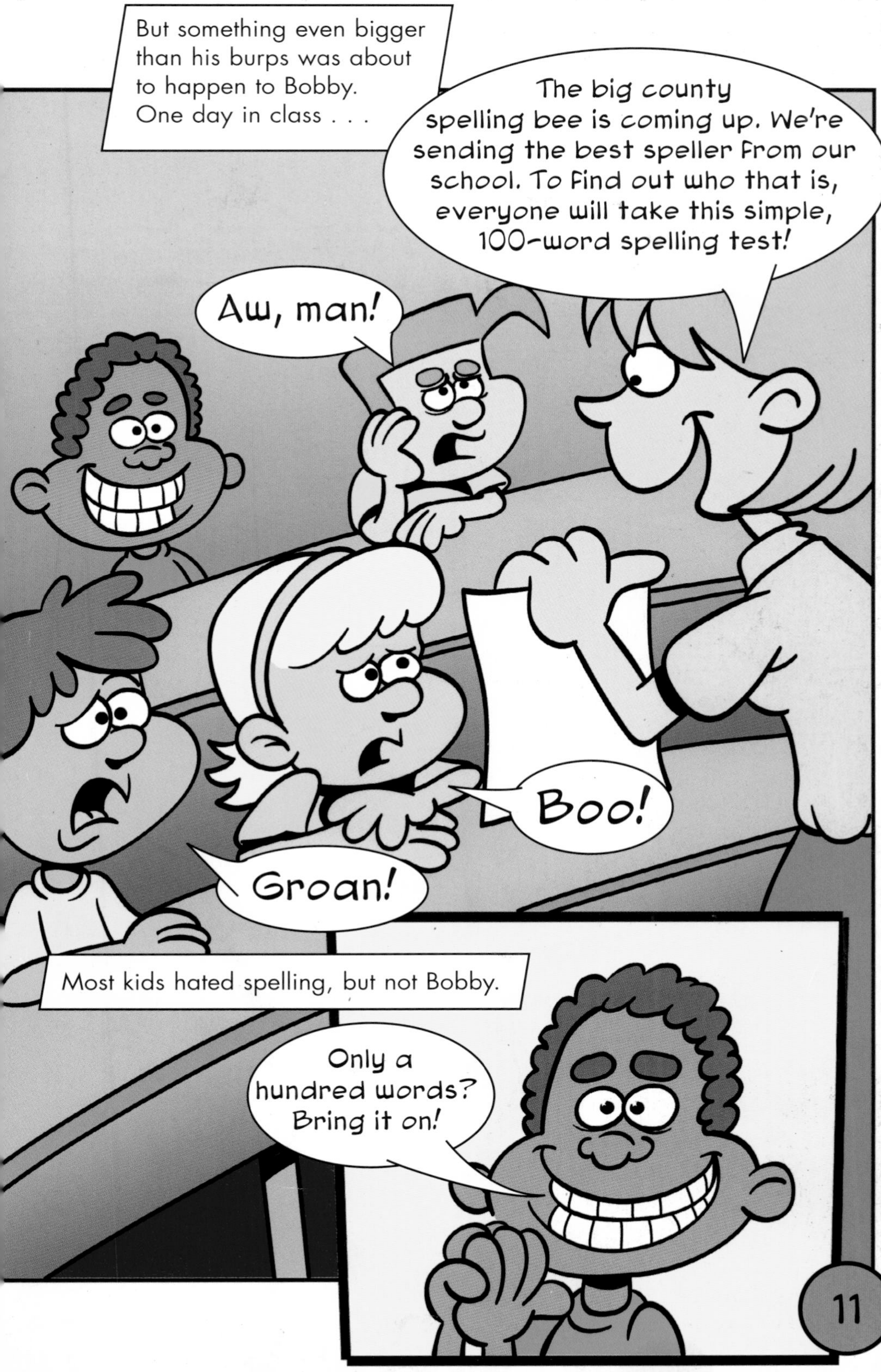

But something even bigger than his burps was about to happen to Bobby. One day in class . . .
The big county spelling bee is coming up. We're sending the best speller from our school. To find out who that is, everyone will take this simple, 100-word spelling test!
Aw, man!
Boo!
Groan!
Most kids hated spelling, but not Bobby.
Only a hundred words? Bring it on!

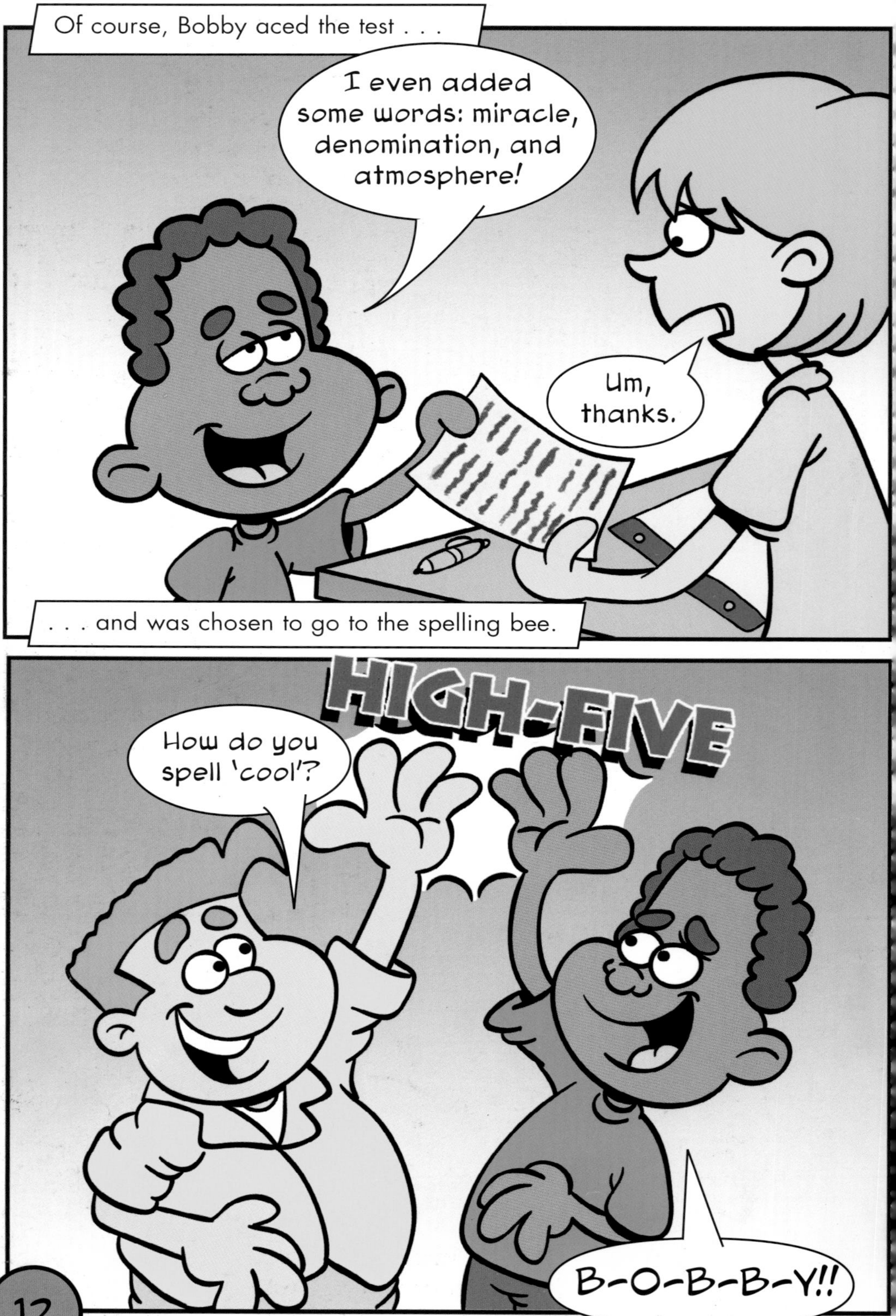
Of course, Bobby aced the test . . .
I even added some words: miracle, denomination, and atmosphere!
Um, thanks.
. . . and was chosen to go to the spelling bee.
HIGH-FIVE
How do you spell 'cool'?
B-O-B-B-Y!!

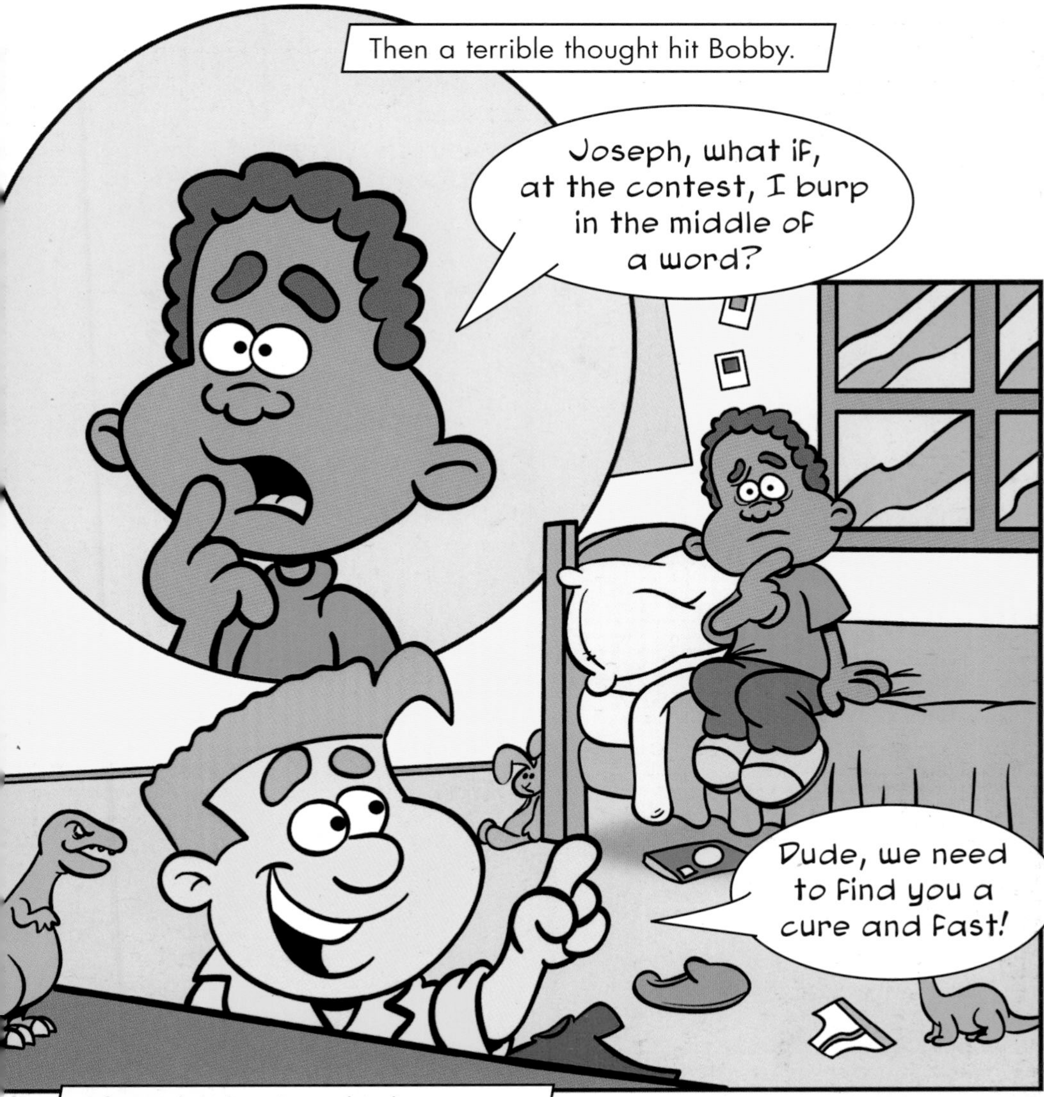
Then a terrible thought hit Bobby.
Joseph, what if, at the contest, I burp in the middle of a word?
Dude, we need to find you a cure and fast!

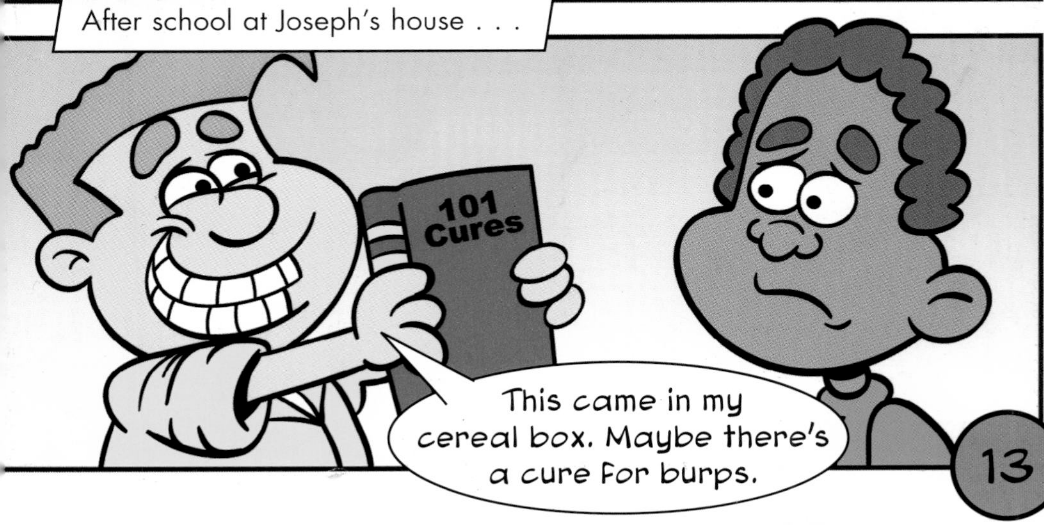
After school at Joseph's house . . .
101 Cures
This came in my cereal box. Maybe there's a cure for burps.

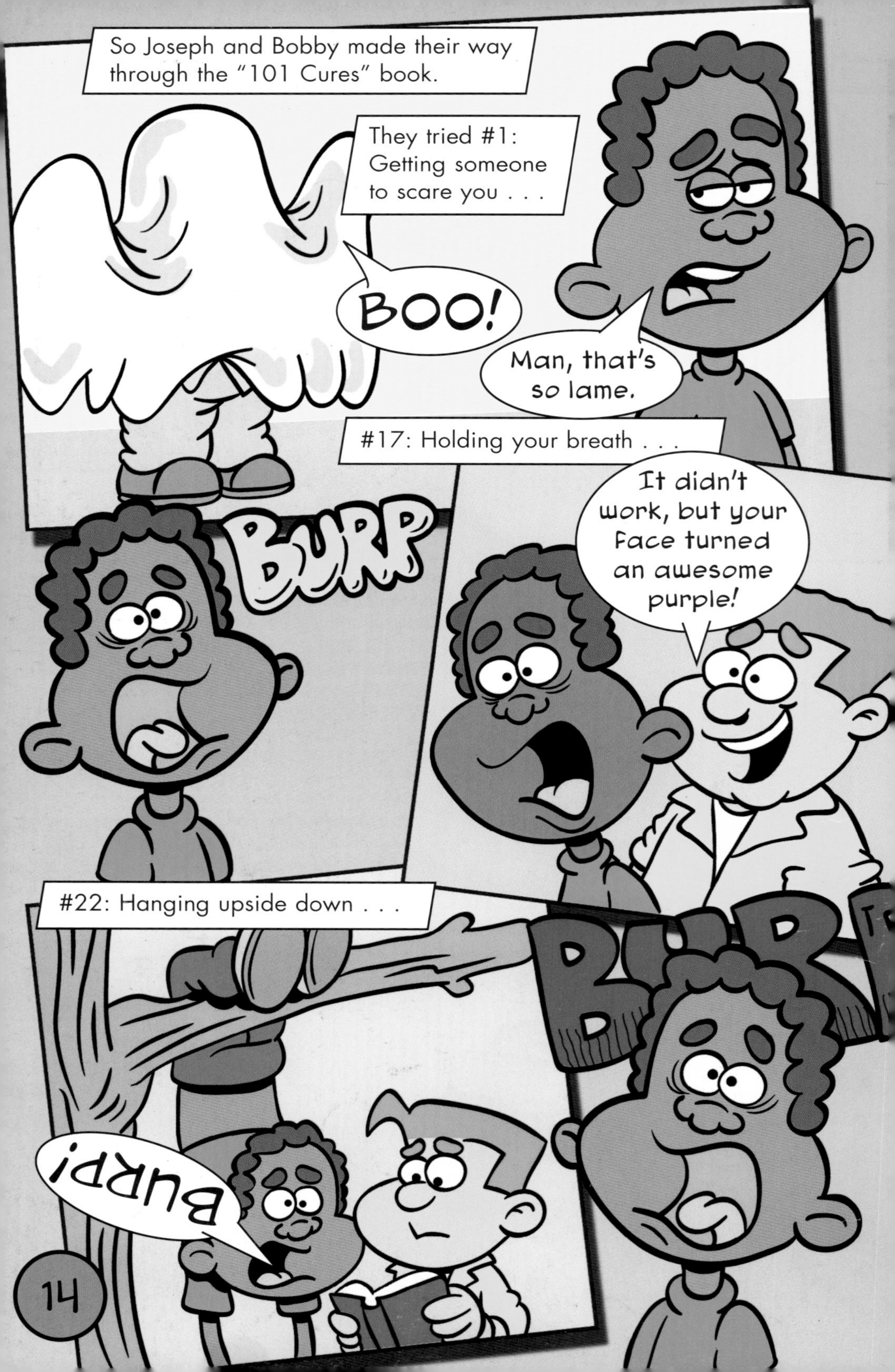

So Joseph and Bobby made their way through the "101 Cures" book.
They tried #1: Getting someone to scare you . . .
BOO!
Man, that's so lame.
#17: Holding your breath . . .
BURP
It didn't work, but your face turned an awesome purple!
#22: Hanging upside down . . .
BURP!
BURP

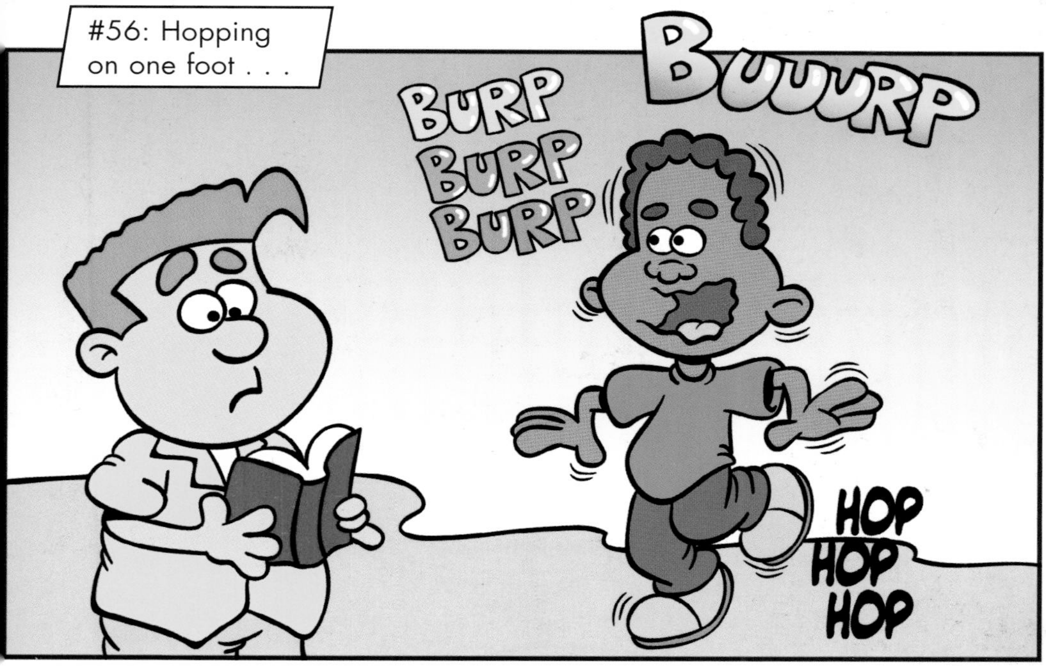
#56: Hopping on one foot . . .
BURP
BURP
BURP
BUUURP
HOP
HOP
HOP

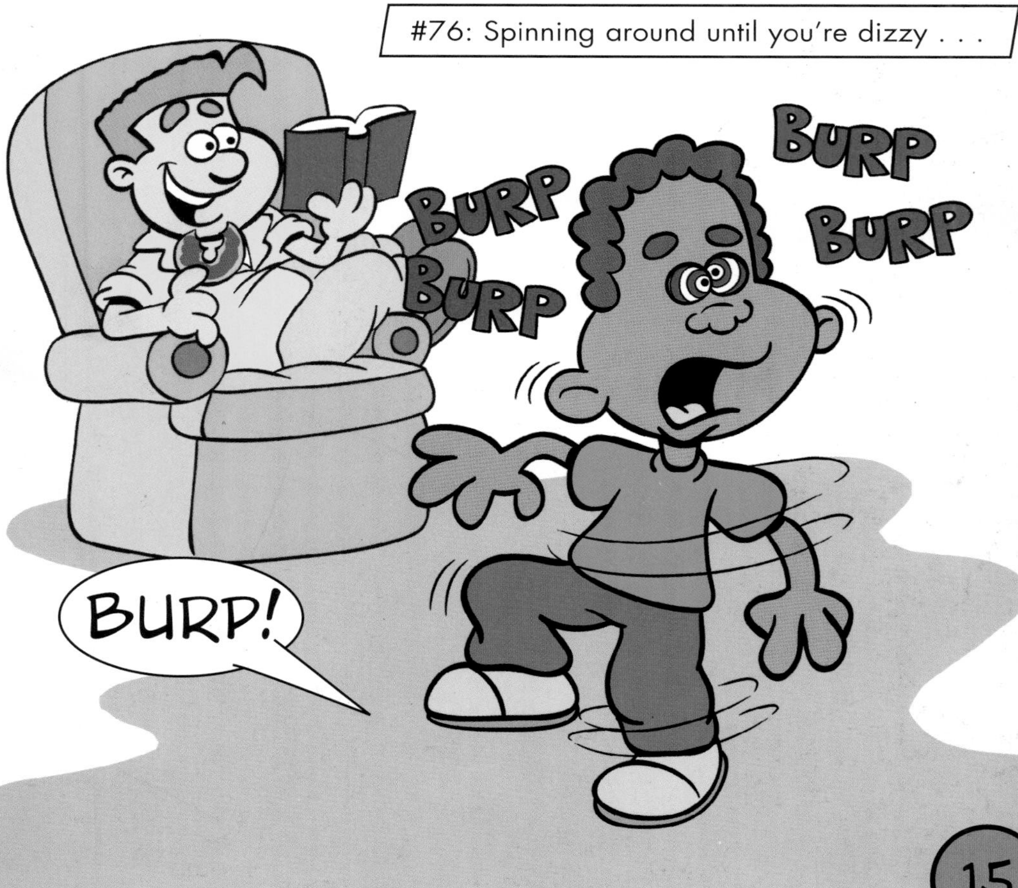
#76: Spinning around until you're dizzy . . .
BURP
BURP
BURP
BURP
BURP!

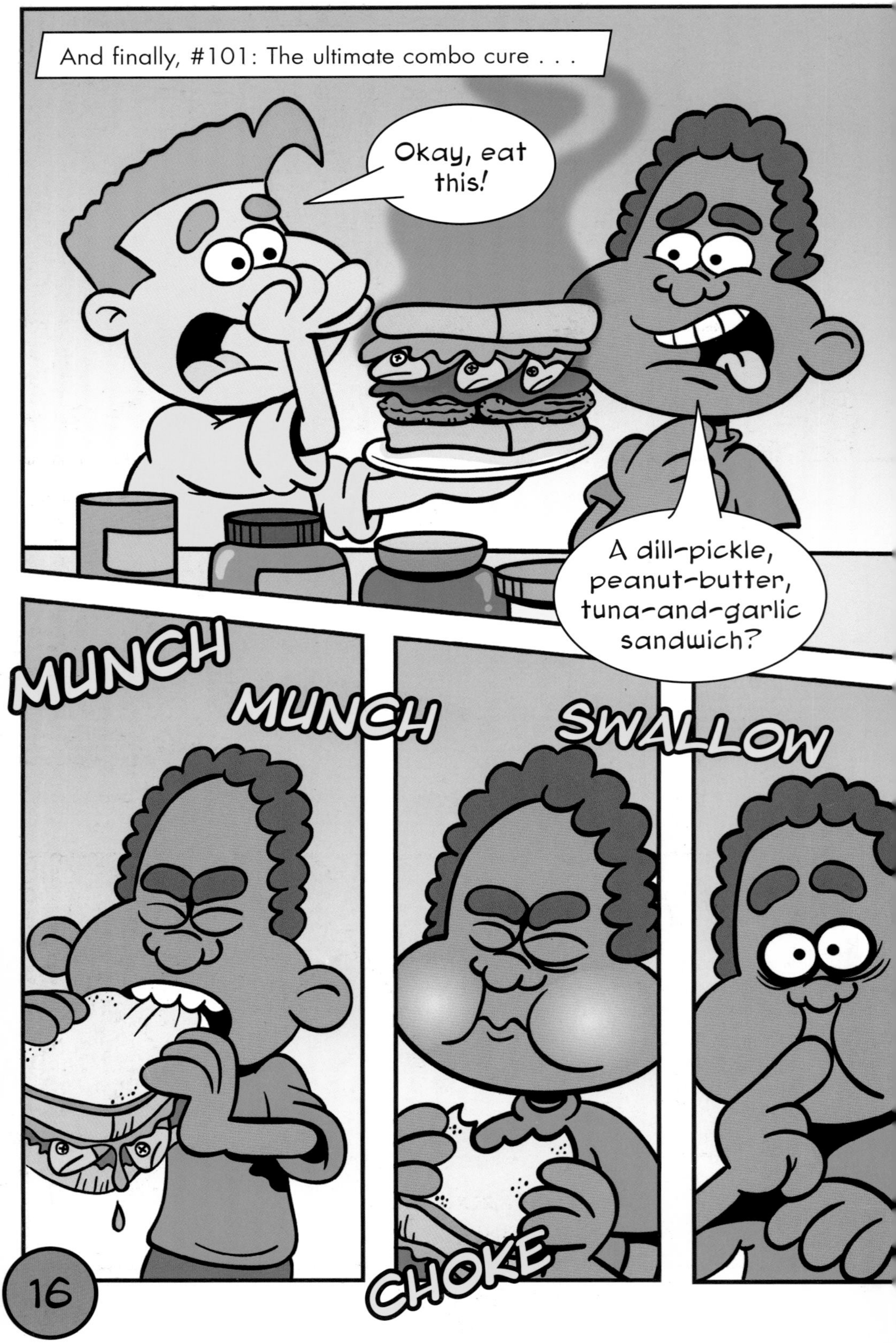
And finally, #101: The ultimate combo cure . . .
Okay, eat this!
A dill-pickle, peanut-butter, tuna-and-garlic sandwich?
MUNCH
MUNCH
SWALLOW
CHOKE

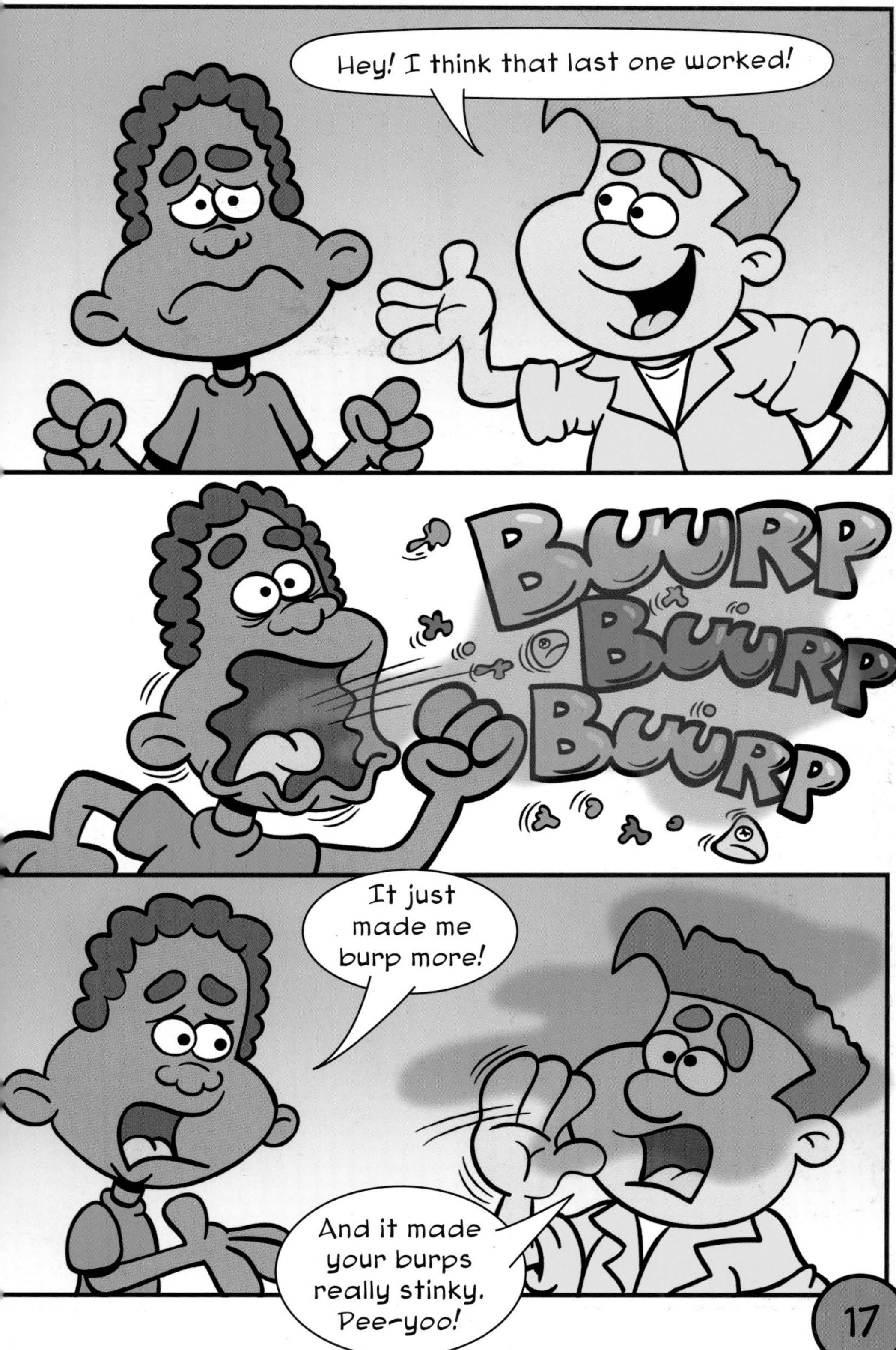
Hey! I think that last one worked!
BUURP
BUURP
BUURP
It just made me burp more!
And it made your burps really stinky. Pee-yoo!

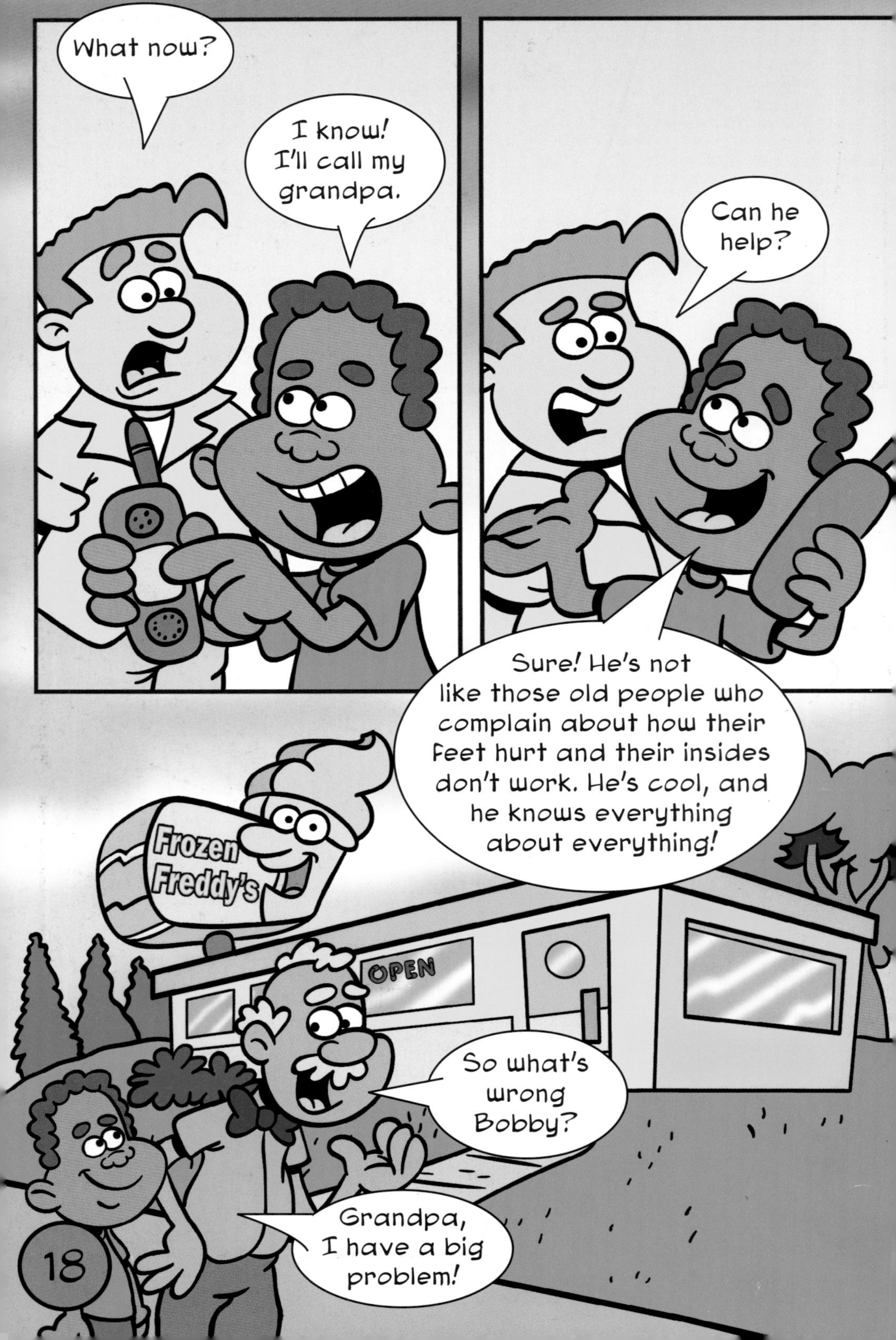
What now?
I know! I'll call my grandpa.
Can he help?
Sure! He's not like those old people who complain about how their feet hurt and their insides don't work. He's cool, and he knows everything about everything!
Frozen Freddy's
OPEN
So what's wrong Bobby?
Grandpa, I have a big problem!

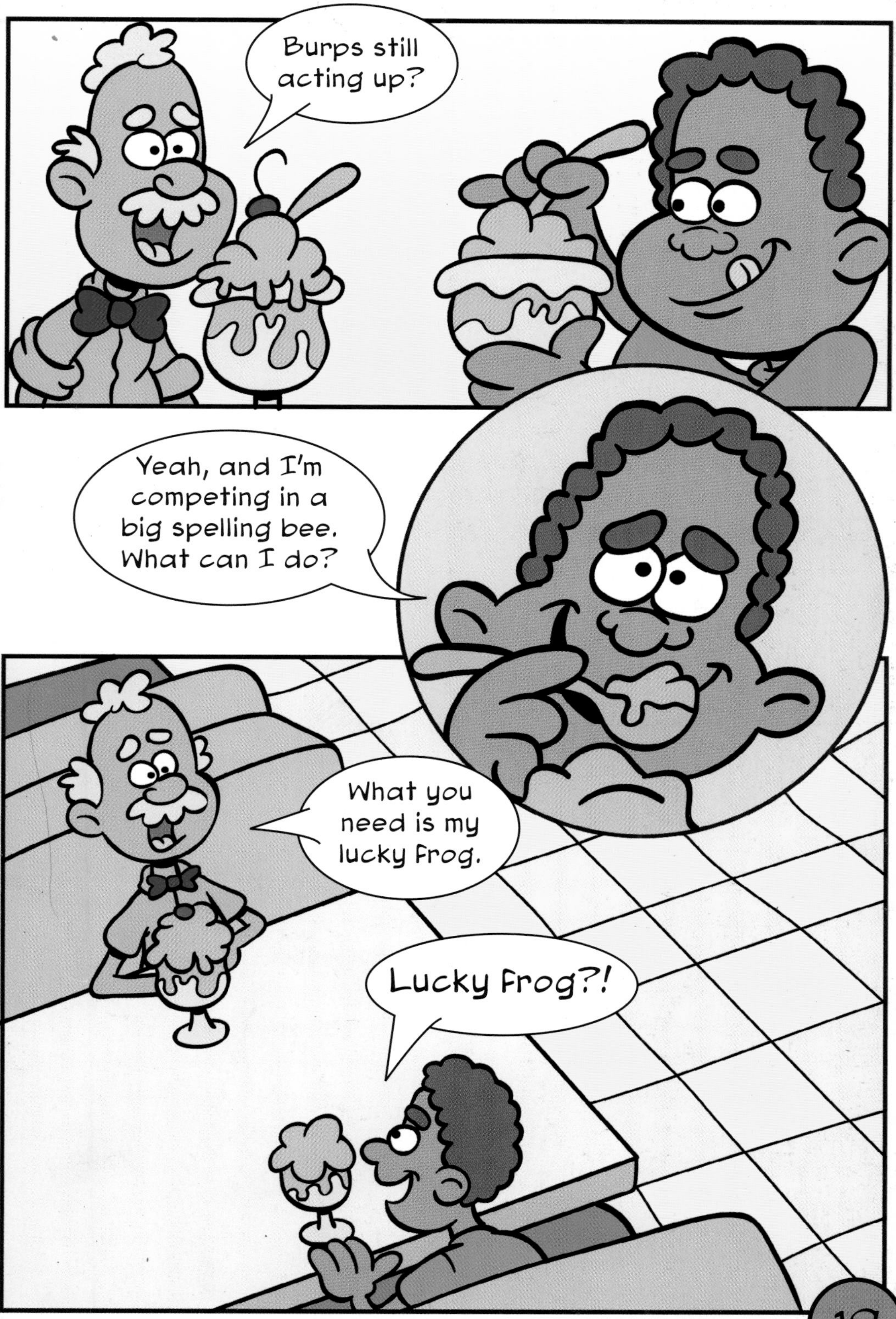
Burps still acting up?
Yeah, and I'm competing in a big spelling bee. What can I do?
What you need is my lucky frog.
Lucky frog?!

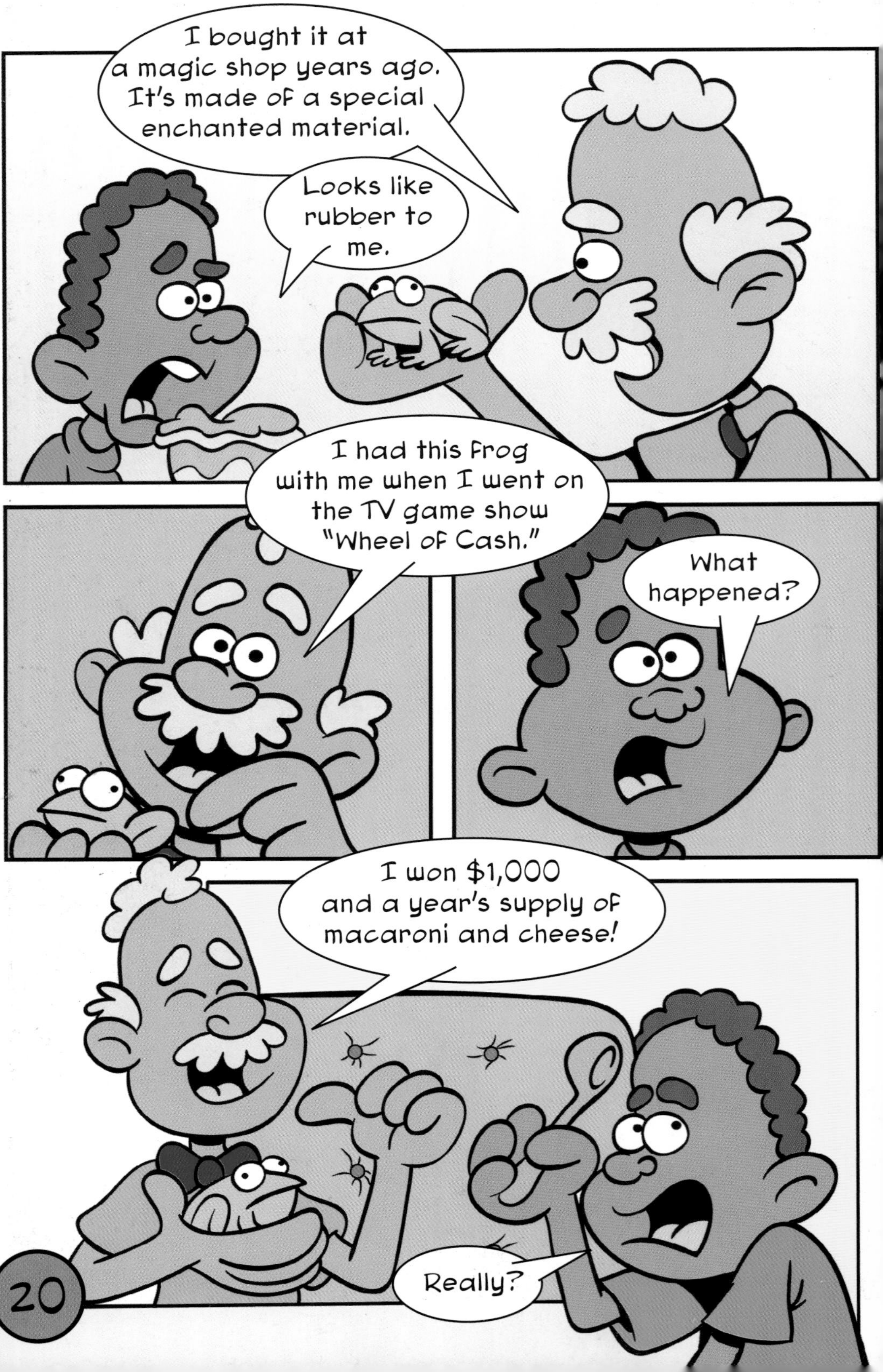
I bought it at a magic shop years ago. It's made of a special enchanted material.
Looks like rubber to me.
I had this frog with me when I went on the TV game show "Wheel of Cash."
What happened?
I won $1,000 and a year's supply of macaroni and cheese!
Really?

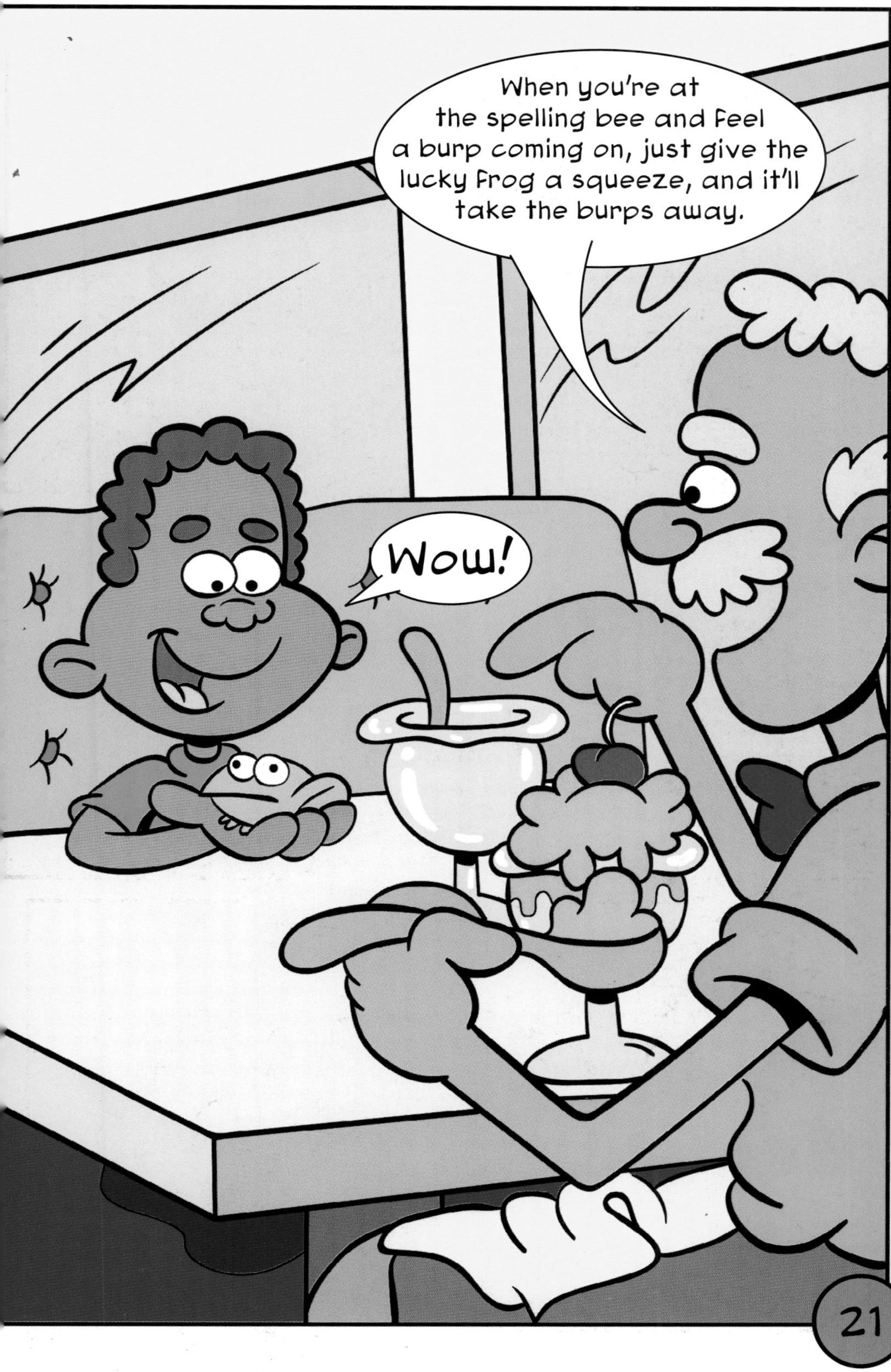
When you're at the spelling bee and feel a burp coming on, just give the lucky frog a squeeze, and it'll take the burps away.
Wow!

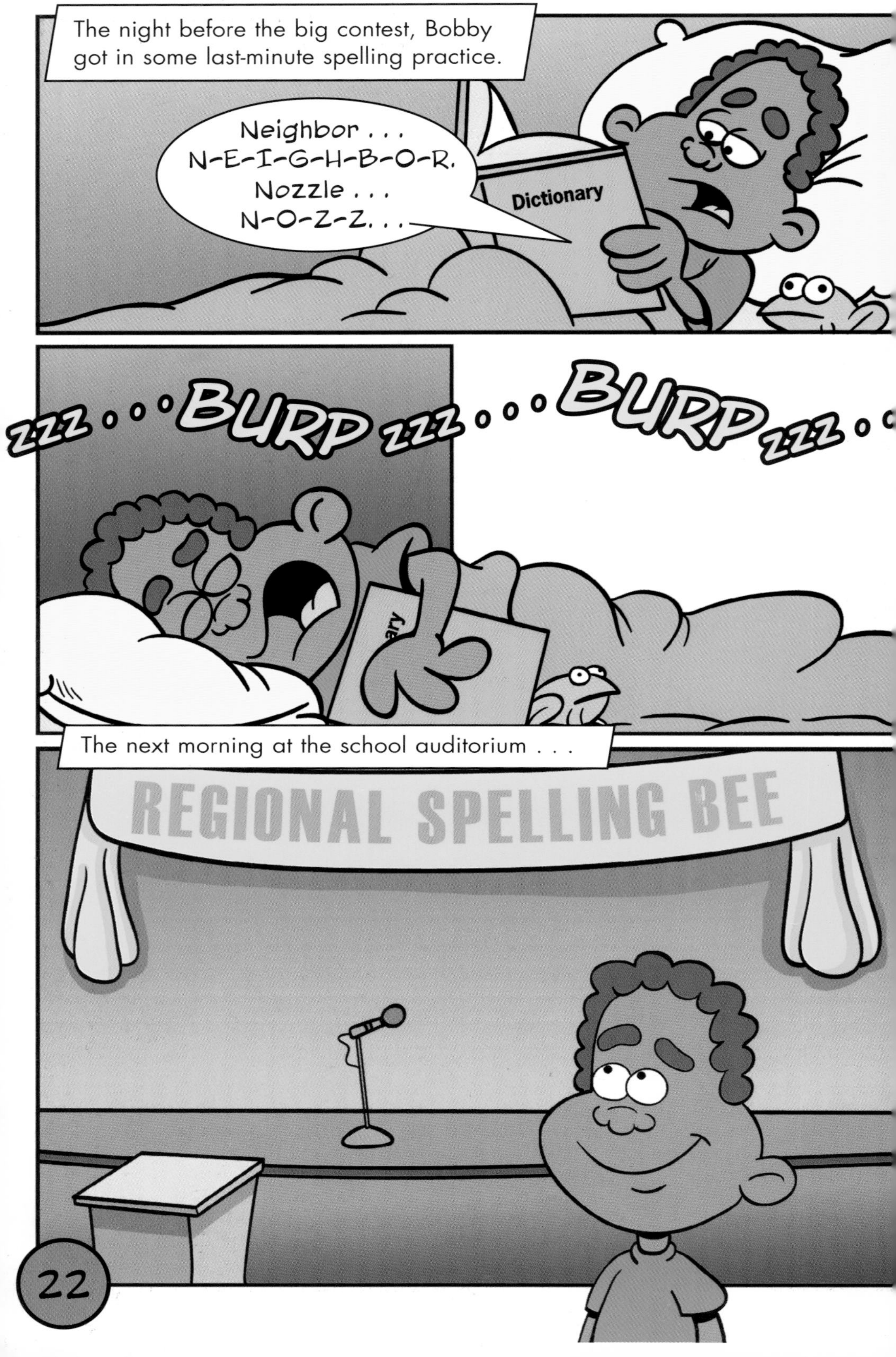
The night before the big contest, Bobby got in some last-minute spelling practice.
Neighbor . . . N-E-I-G-H-B-O-R. Nozzle . . . N-O-Z-Z. . .
Dictionary
zzz . . . BURP zzz . . . BURP zzz . . .
The next morning at the school auditorium . . .
REGIONAL SPELLING BEE

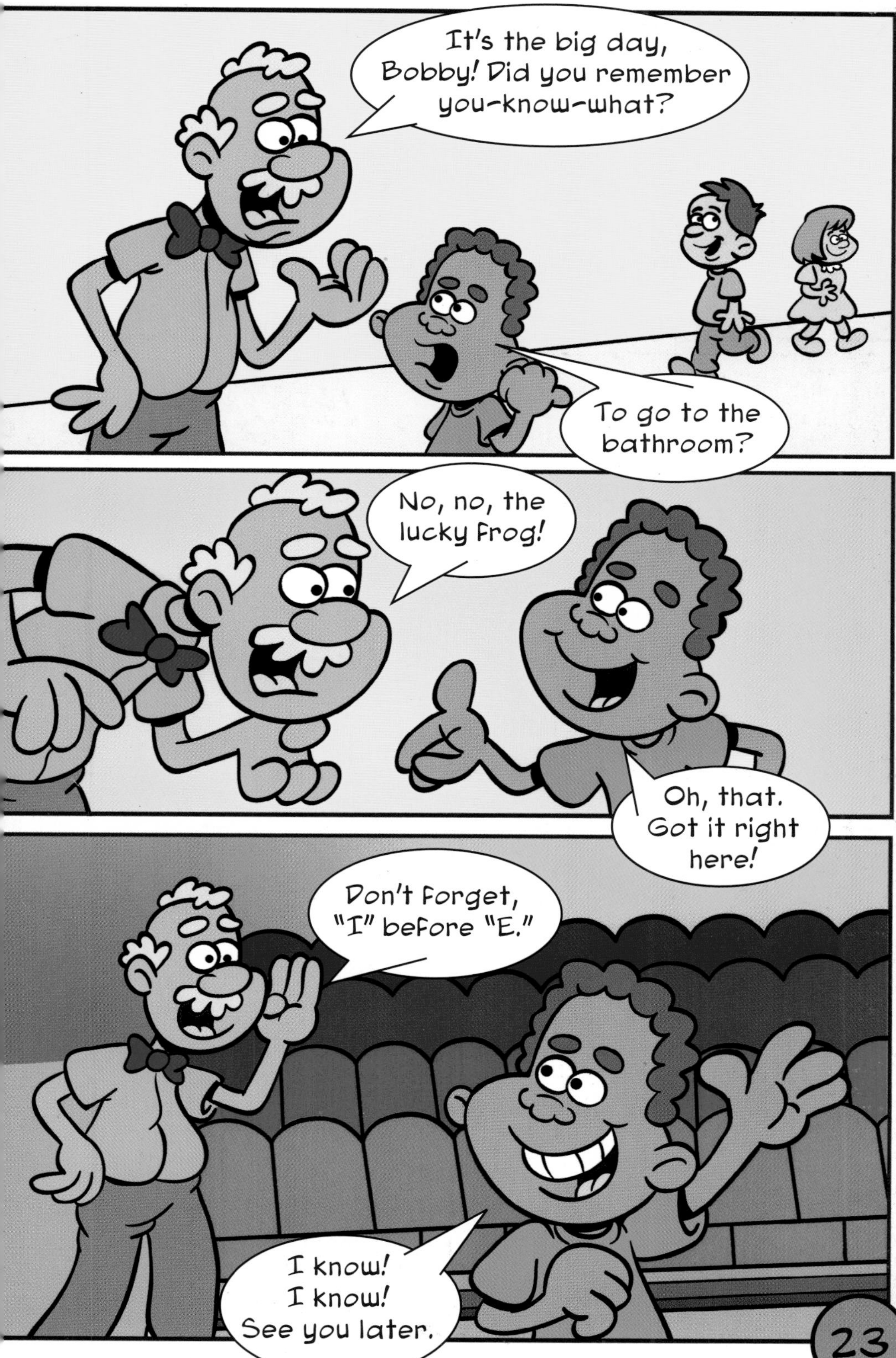
It's the big day, Bobby! Did you remember you-know-what?
To go to the bathroom?
No, no, the lucky frog!
Oh, that. Got it right here!
Don't forget, "I" before "E."
I know! I know! See you later.

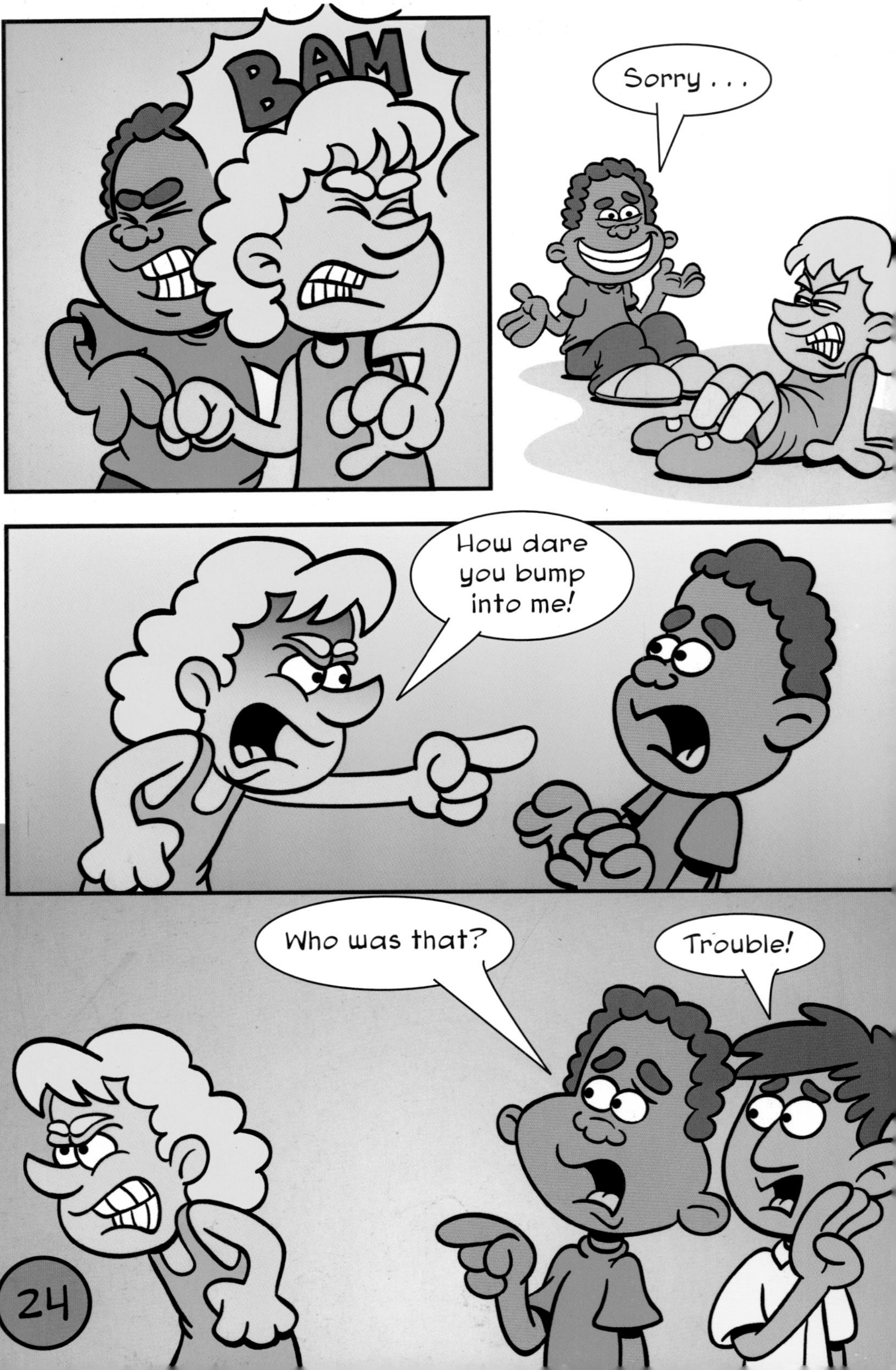
BAM
Sorry . . .
How dare you bump into me!
Who was that?
Trouble!

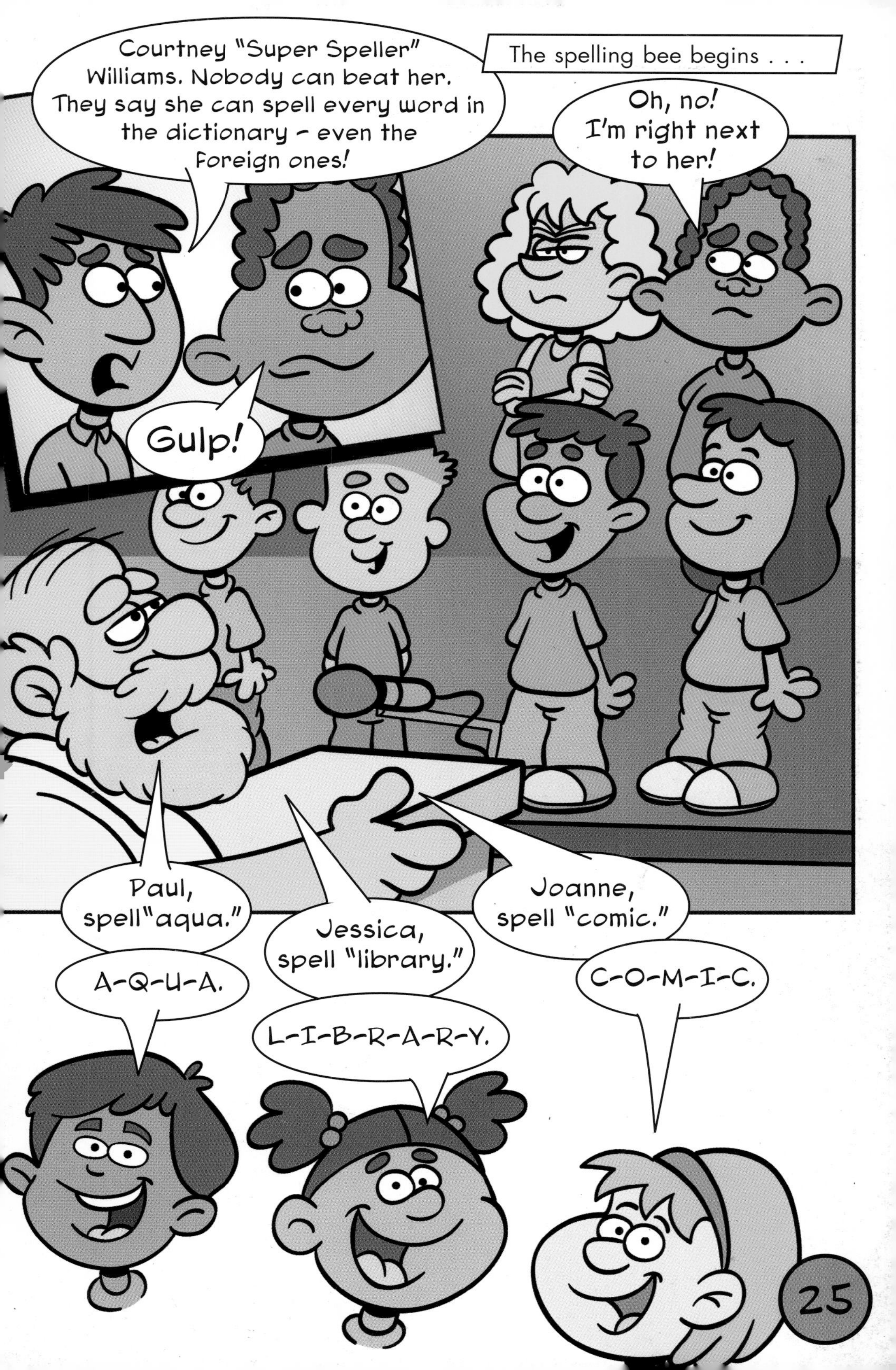
The spelling bee begins . . .
Courtney "Super Speller" Williams. Nobody can beat her. They say she can spell every word in the dictionary - even the foreign ones!
Gulp!
Oh, no! I'm right next to her!
Paul, spell"aqua."
A-Q-U-A.
Jessica, spell "library."
L-I-B-R-A-R-Y.
Joanne, spell "comic."
C-O-M-I-C.
25

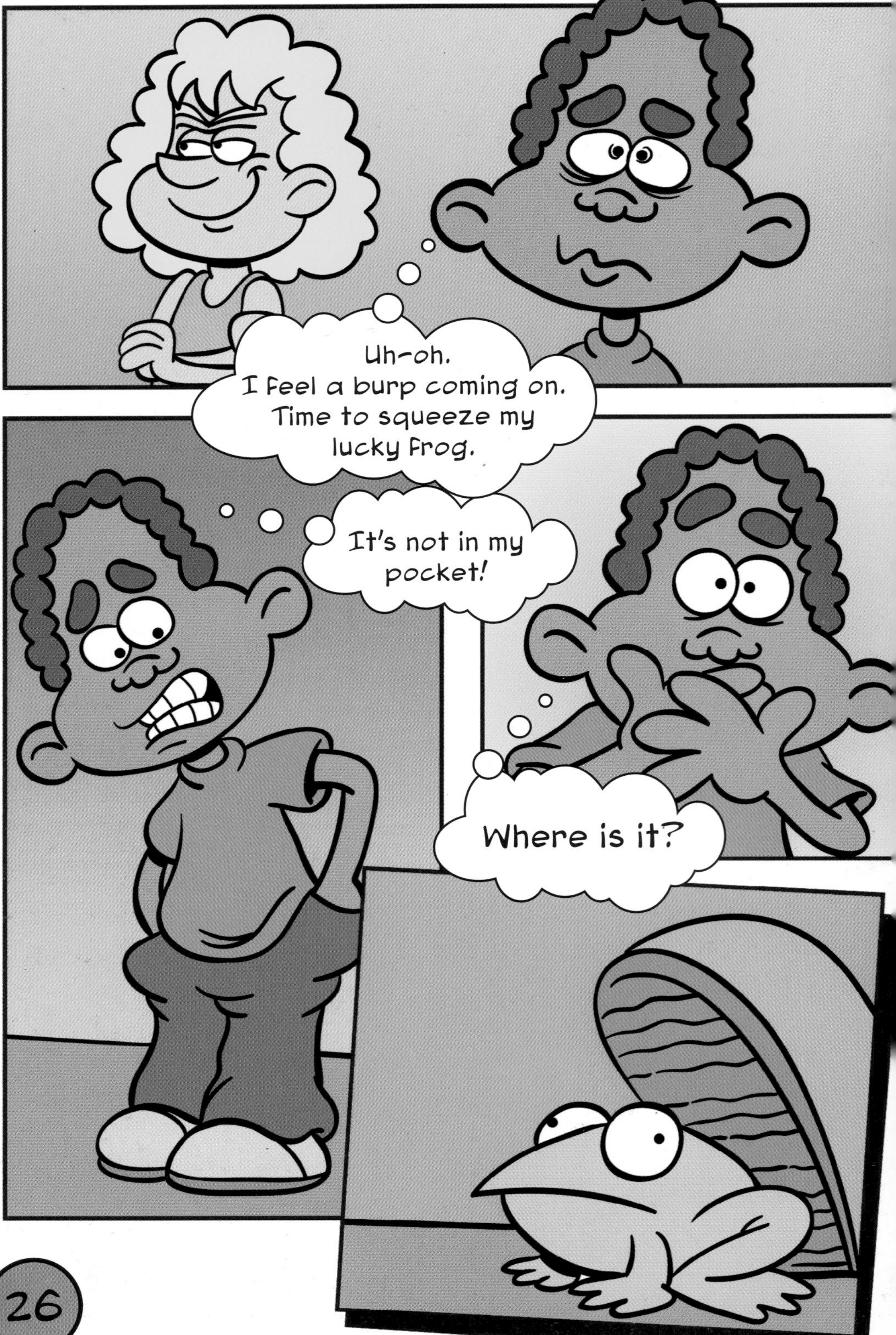
Uh-oh.
I feel a burp coming on.
Time to squeeze my
lucky frog.
It's not in my
pocket!
Where is it?

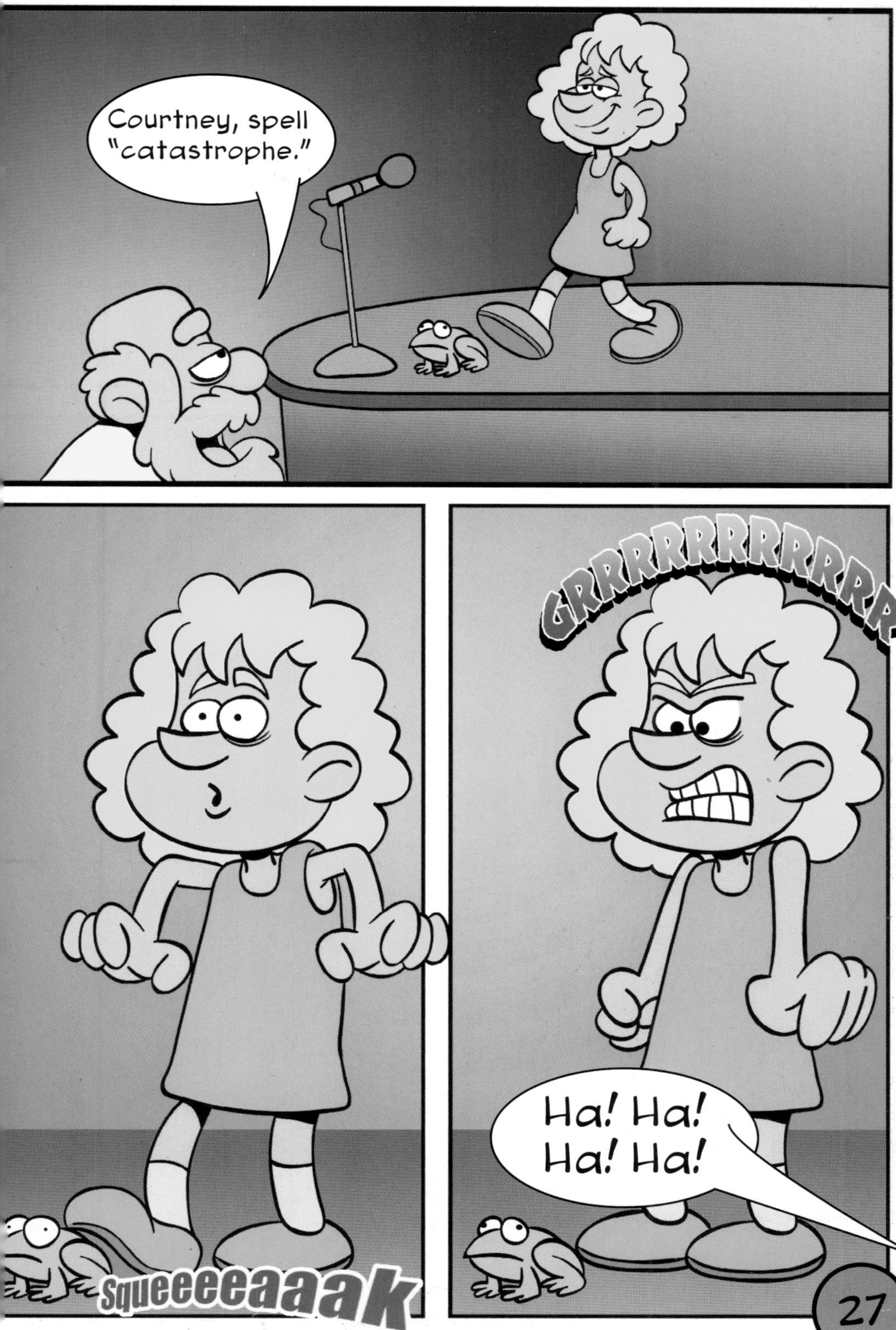
Courtney, spell "catastrophe."
Squeeeeeaaaak
GRRRRRRRRRRRR
Ha! Ha!
Ha! Ha!

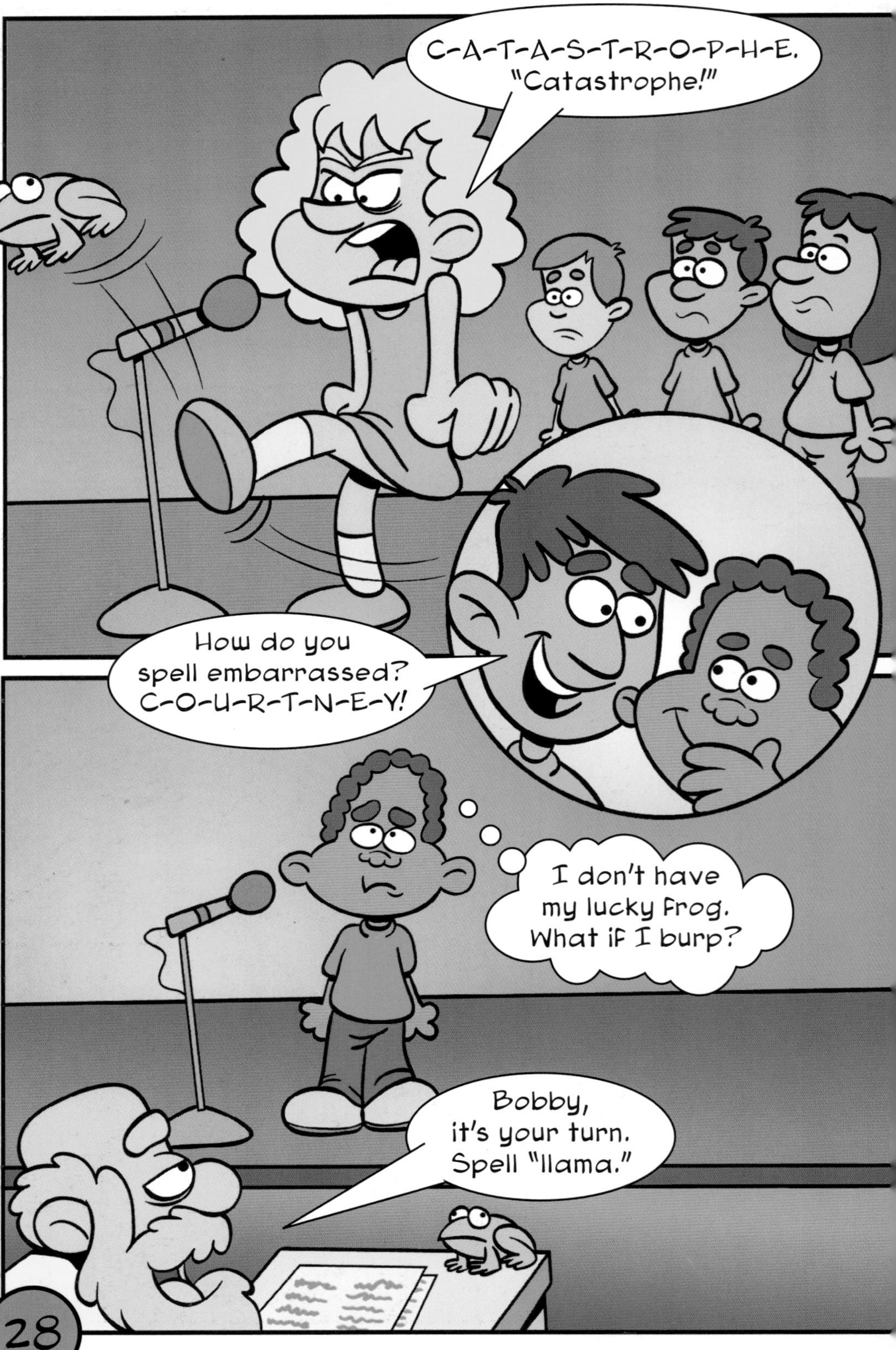
C-A-T-A-S-T-R-O-P-H-E. "Catastrophe!"
How do you spell embarrassed? C-O-U-R-T-N-E-Y!
I don't have my lucky frog. What if I burp?
Bobby, it's your turn. Spell "llama."

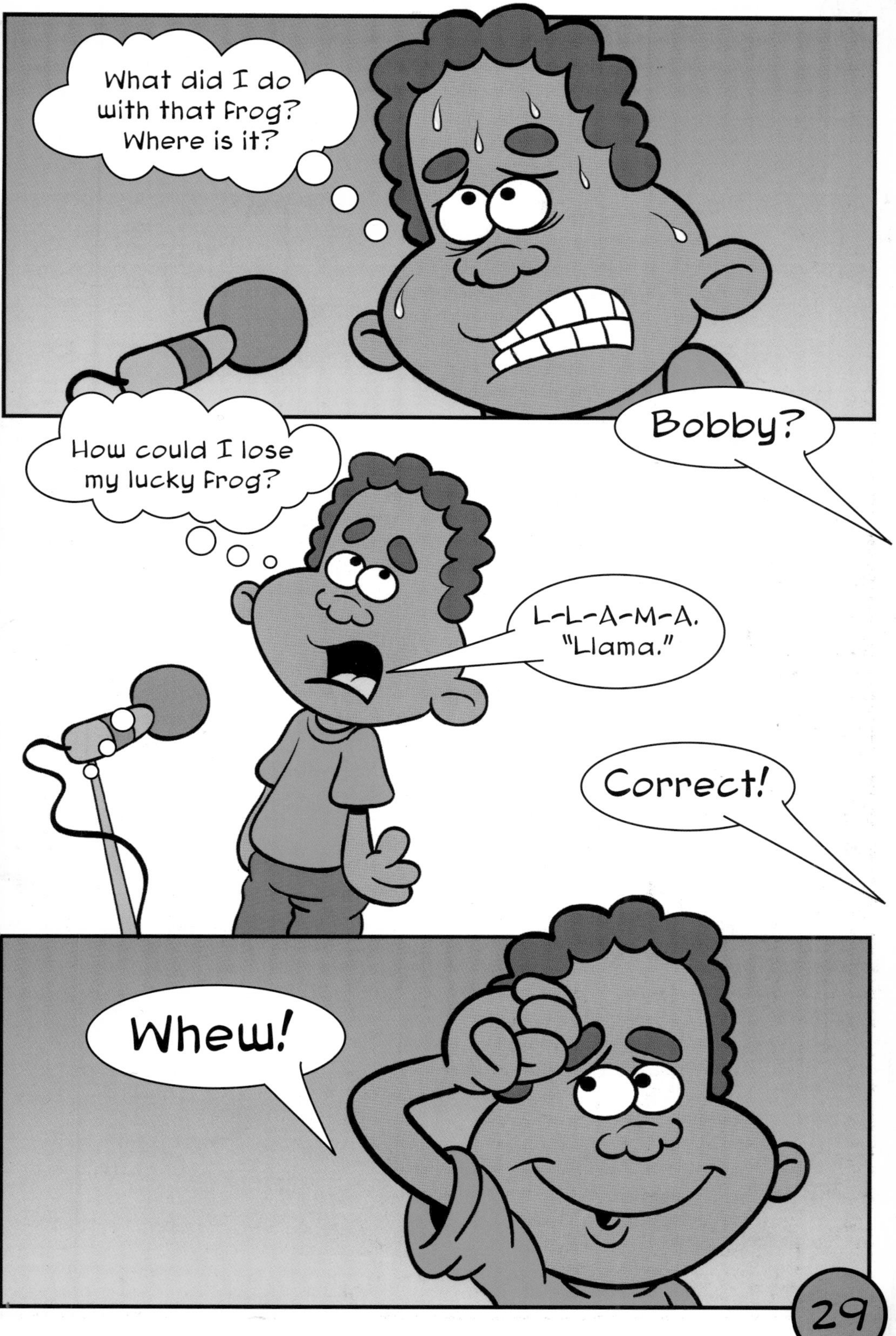
What did I do with that frog? Where is it?
How could I lose my lucky frog?
Bobby?
L-L-A-M-A. "Llama."
Correct!
Whew!

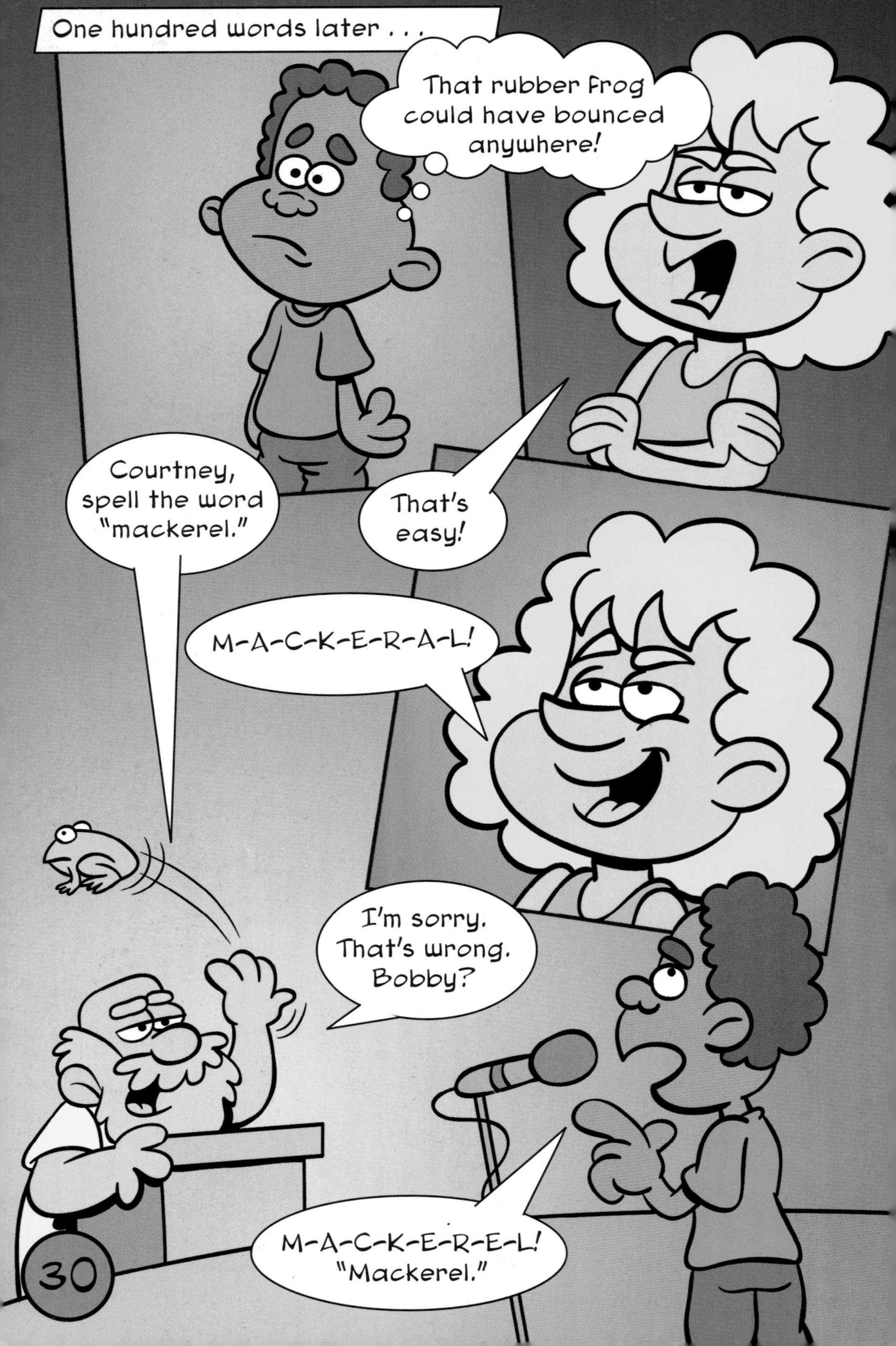
One hundred words later . . .
That rubber frog could have bounced anywhere!
That's easy!
Courtney, spell the word "mackerel."
M-A-C-K-E-R-A-L!
I'm sorry. That's wrong. Bobby?
M-A-C-K-E-R-E-L! "Mackerel."

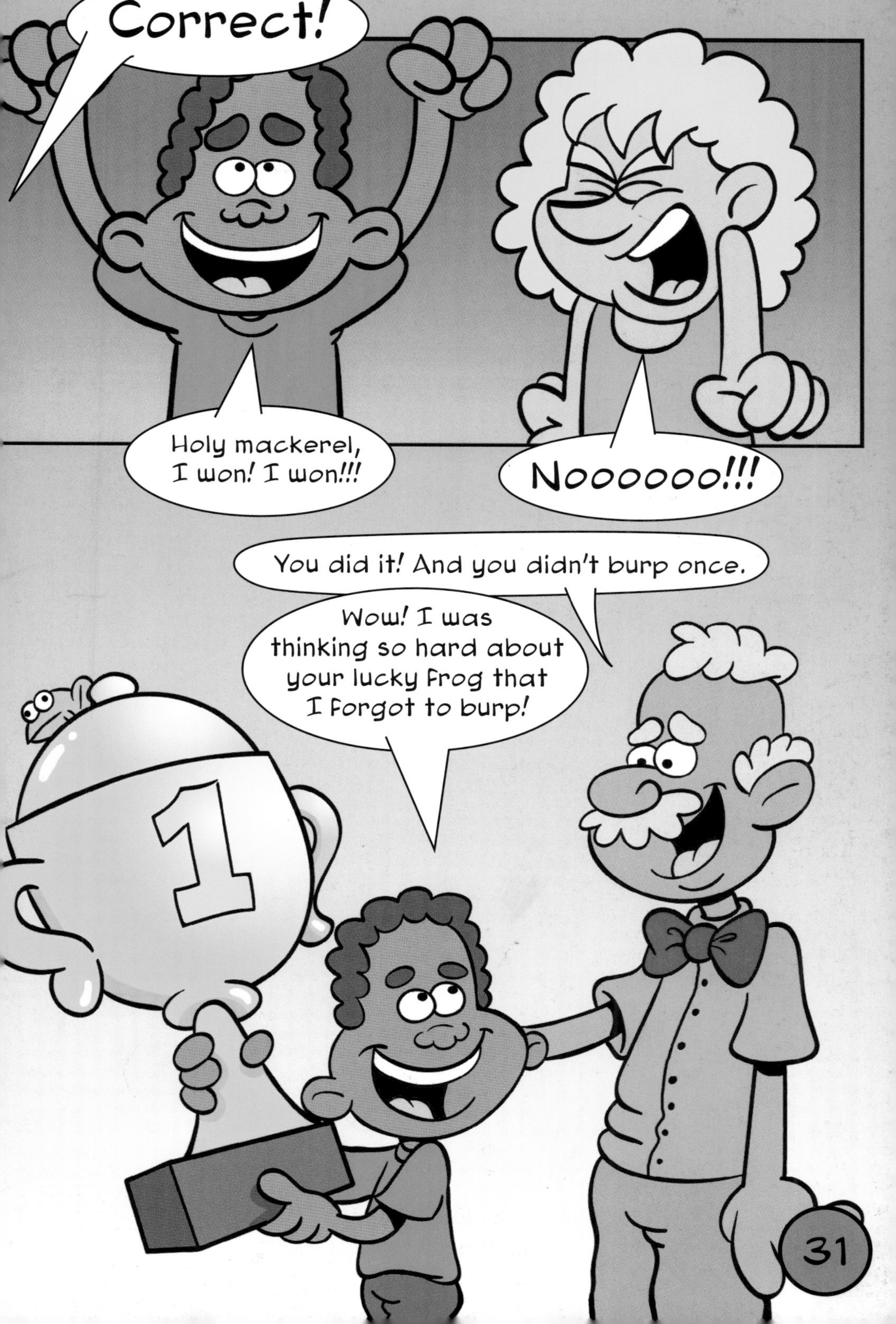
Correct!
Holy mackerel, I won! I won!!!
Noooooo!!!
You did it! And you didn't burp once.
Wow! I was thinking so hard about your lucky frog that I forgot to burp!
1

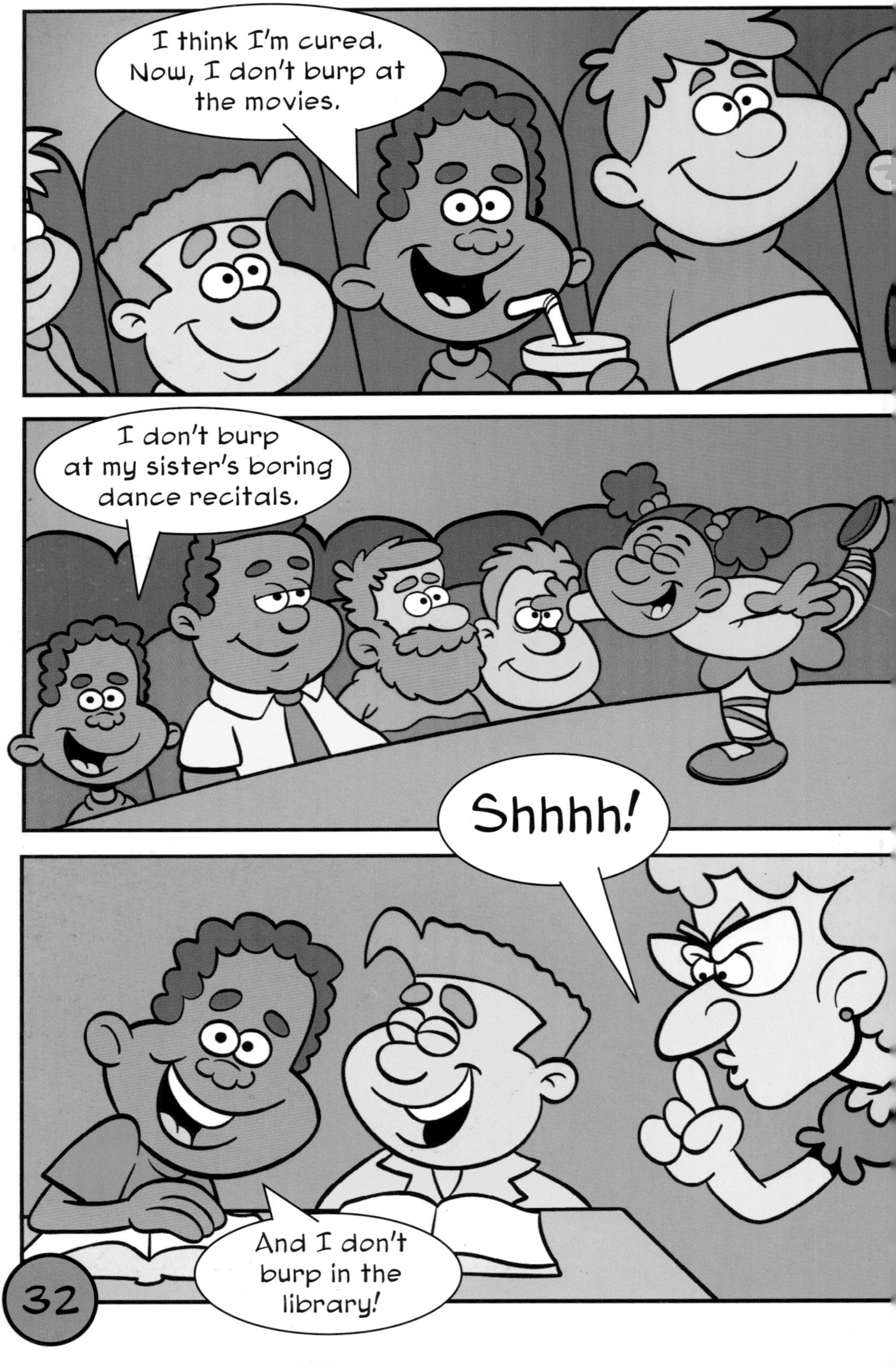
I think I'm cured. Now, I don't burp at the movies.
I don't burp at my sister's boring dance recitals.
Shhhh!
And I don't burp in the library!

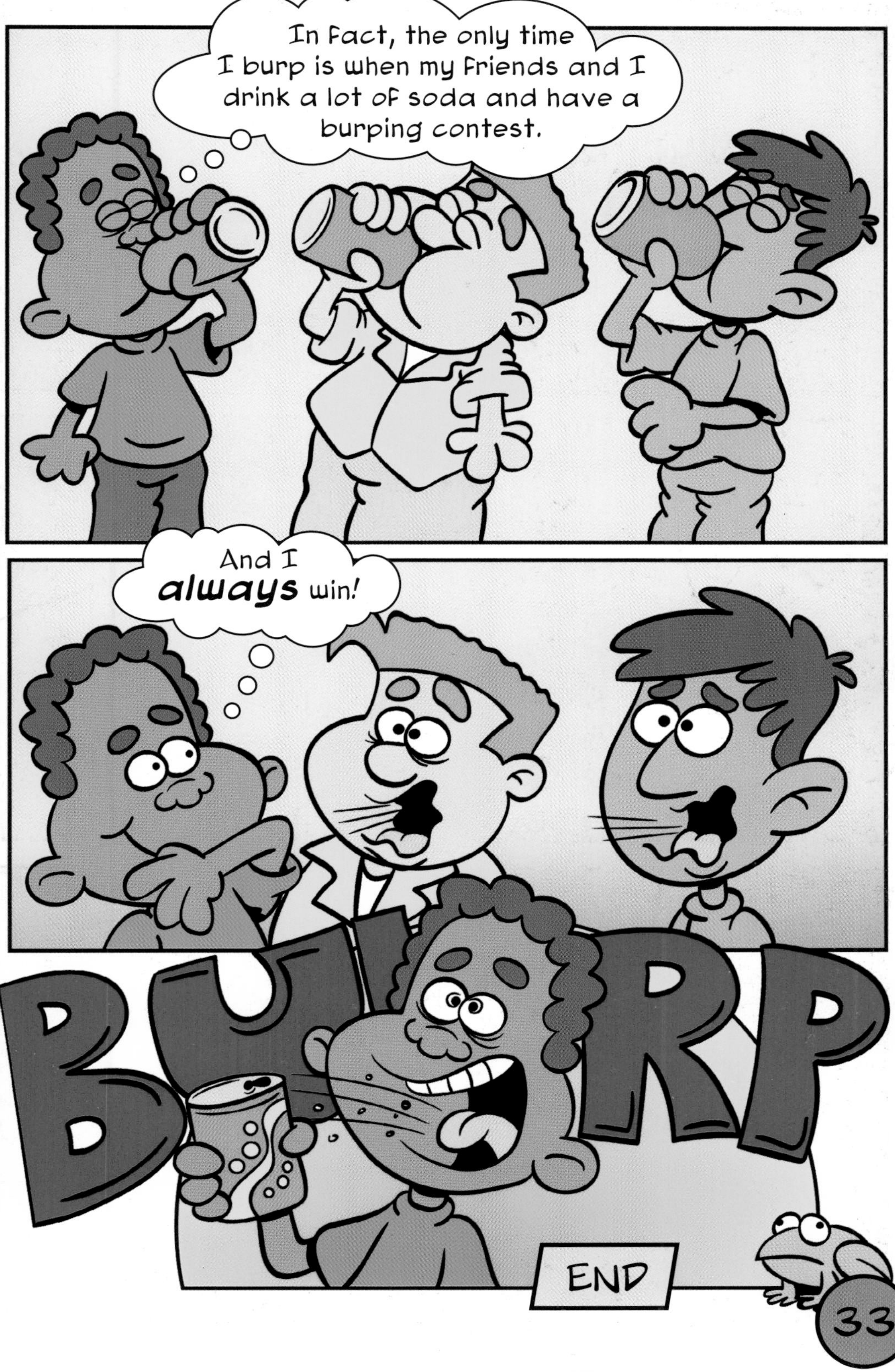

In fact, the only time I burp is when my friends and I drink a lot of soda and have a burping contest.
And I **always** win!
BURP
END

ABOUT THE AUTHOR

Scott Nickel has written children's books, short fiction for *Boys' Life Magazine*, humorous greeting cards, and lots of really funny knock-knock jokes. Scott is also the author of many Garfield books.

Currently, Scott lives in Indiana with his wife, two sons, four cats, a parakeet, and several sea monkeys.

ABOUT THE ILLUSTRATOR

Steve Harpster has loved drawing funny cartoons, mean monsters, and goofy gadgets since he was able to pick up a pencil. In first grade, he was able to avoid his writing assignments by working on the pictures for stories instead.

Steve landed a job drawing funny pictures for books, and that's really what he's best at. Steve lives in Columbus, Ohio, with his wonderful wife, Karen, and their sheepdog, Doodle.

GLOSSARY

aqua (AH-kwa) water or the color greenish-blue; not to be confused with the Spanish word agua, which also means "water"

catastrophe (kuh-TASS-truh-fee) a disaster or a terrible event, such as losing your lucky rubber frog during a spelling bee or burping a tuna-fish sandwich out your nose

llama (LAH-muh) a large, camel-like mammal that lives in South America

mackerel (MAK-ur-uhl) a shiny blue fish that lives in the ocean; eating too much mackerel can make you burp. Fish burps! Now that's a real catastrophe.

spelling bee (SPEL-ing BEE) a contest where people have to spell words correctly, such as the word "correctly"

Read it! Read it!

BURP BLURBS

Burps are caused by something you can't even see – air. The average person swallows a cup of air a day. Some people swallow as much as 10 cups a day!

Foods release gas in your stomach. Gas can make you burp, too. Foods that contain the most gas are milk, apples, nuts, onions, sauerkraut, and soda pop.

When you are nervous, you swallow more air than normal. Then you burp!

When the air or gas in your stomach escapes through your mouth, you start burping. Doctors call it by a bigger name. They say you are **ERUCTATING** (uh-RUK-tay-ting).

The world's loudest burp was recorded at more than 118 decibels (DESS-uh-buhls). That's louder than the buzz of a chain saw!.

The best way to prevent burping is to stop swallowing so much air. Here are some real-life cures for preventing or getting rid of burps.

1.) Don't drink fizzy drinks, like soda pop.

2.) Don't use a straw when you drink.

3.) Don't gulp down liquids. Sip them slowly.

4.) Chew with your mouth closed.

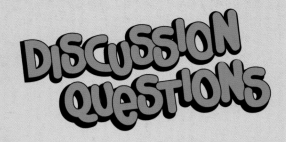

1.) Bobby burps everywhere. Do you think he
    really can't help it, or is he making excuses?

2.) Bobby's grandpa gives him his lucky frog to
    help him stop burping. Do you think the frog
    was really lucky, or was Grandpa
    only pretending?

3.) Courtney was upset when she stepped on
    Bobby's frog on the stage. Did that make
    her lose the spelling bee? Who do you think
    is the better speller?

WRITING PROMPTS

1.) Bobby's burps make a lot of noise! Write a story describing a strange or funny sound that you can make with your mouth, and the trouble it gets you into.

2.) Grandpa's lucky frog helped him win a year's supply of macaroni and cheese. Write a story that tells how you win a contest and what the prize is.

3.) Bobby's friend tries to help him stop burping. What if you couldn't stop burping, either? Write down what your friends would do to try and cure you. Do any of the cures work?

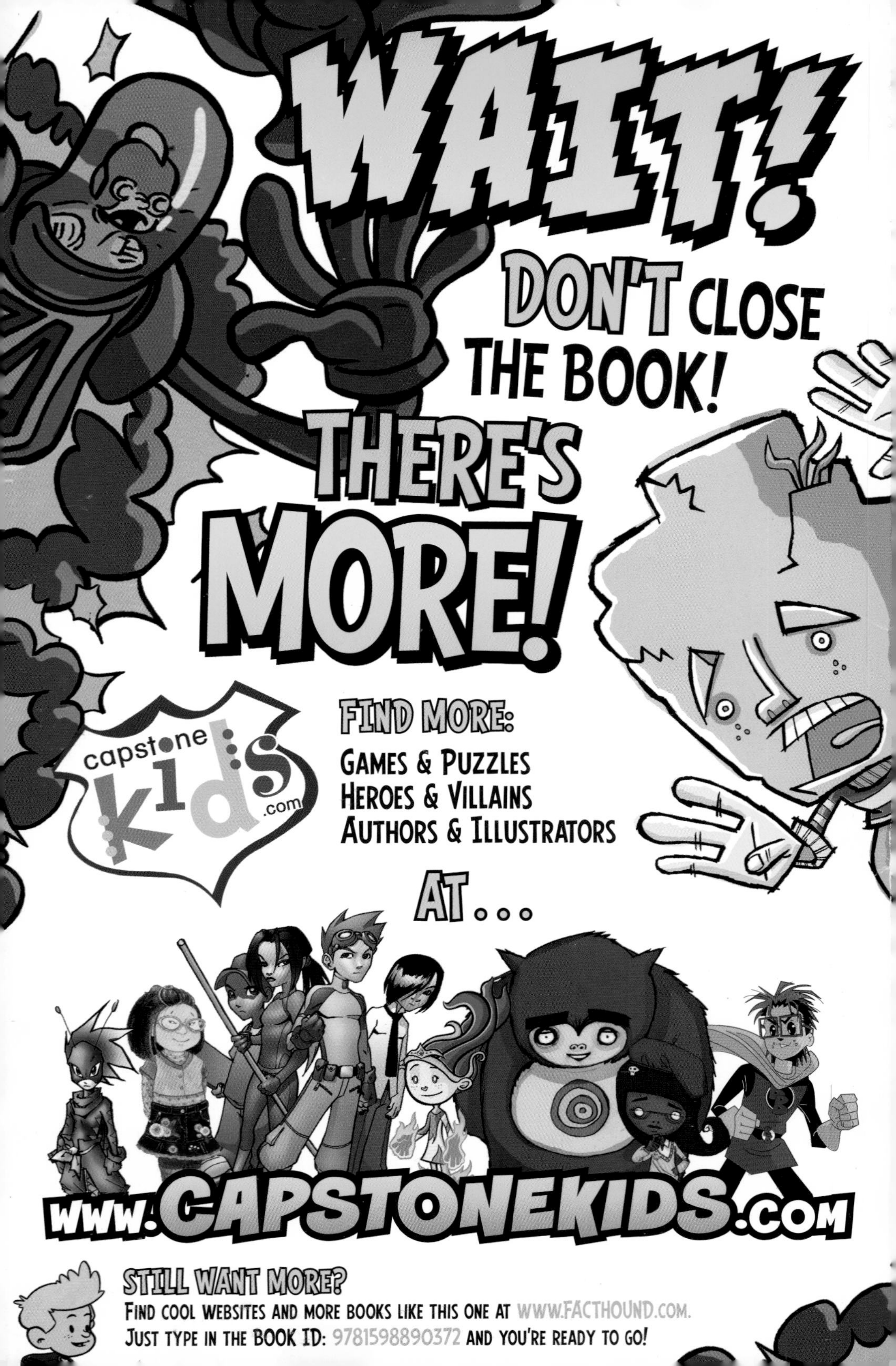
WAIT!
DON'T CLOSE THE BOOK!
THERE'S MORE!
capstone kids .com
FIND MORE:
GAMES & PUZZLES
HEROES & VILLAINS
AUTHORS & ILLUSTRATORS
AT...
WWW.CAPSTONEKIDS.COM
STILL WANT MORE?
FIND COOL WEBSITES AND MORE BOOKS LIKE THIS ONE AT WWW.FACTHOUND.COM.
JUST TYPE IN THE BOOK ID: 9781598890372 AND YOU'RE READY TO GO!